Written Out

HOWARD MITTELMARK

Written Out

THE PERMANENT PRESS
Sag Harbor, NY 11963

For information, address:
    The Permanent Press
    4170 Noyac Road
    Sag Harbor, NY 11963
    www.thepermanentpress.com

Library of Congress Cataloging-in-Publication Data

Mittelmark, Howard, author.
    Written out / Howard Mittelmark.
    Sag Harbor, NY: The Permanent Press, 2019.
    ISBN: 978-1-57962-572-6 (hardcover)
    ISBN: 978-1-57962-592-4 (ebook)
        1. Long Island (N.Y.)—Fiction. 2. Noir fiction.

PS3613.I875 W75 2019
813'.6—dc23   2019039241

Printed in the United States of America

For Sandy,
my actual genius novelist wife

CHAPTER ONE

January 2015

I know this sounds overly dramatic, but returning to Long Island was like dying.

Bear with me.

There's a reason people move to New York when they're young, when they believe anything can happen, that magical things are waiting for them, that they're special. For some people it turns out to be true.

Even at my age, New York can have a quality of nascent possibility, the promise of unexpected and unpredictable encounters, whether romantic, artistic, or financial. It can make all of life seem numinous, if only sporadically, a series of choices and options glowing with potential, a forward-moving journey where you don't know what will happen next.

Getting on the train in Penn Station, leaving New York City to move back to the Long Island town where I grew up, was the opposite of that. As the train chugged steadily eastward, getting ever closer to home, it was like a system shutting down, piece by piece, synapse by synapse: the snuffing out of light, of hope, of vision. It was like being forced onto an ever narrower path, with fewer turns and escapes; like crawling ever further into a human lobster trap.

Which, by the way, is the kind of thing you'd think someone who grew up here would be familiar with. A lobster
trap, I mean, what with the stations being announced over
the train's loudspeaker, names like Freeport, and Seaford,
and Melville. But, no. This wasn't a trip to the Long Island
of nineteenth-century whaling towns, nor was I headed to
Fitzgerald's West Egg or the luxe literary Hamptons. I was
slinking back whence I came, to the ratty strip malls of Long
Island's South Shore, to the petit bourgeois, blue-collar suburbs, Levitt's cracker-box split-levels.

I'd run out of options, is the thing, and as Robert Frost
said, home is the place where, when your mother is spending the winter in her condo in Florida and you know where
she hides the key, you can stay until you figure something
out. Or as he might have said in his first draft, assuming
he had a good editor, the value of which is hard to over-
estimate. I know this because I work as an editor, or did,
until the publishing industry decided it could do just fine
without me.

Now, here I was, getting off the LIRR at the Seaford train
station, homeless, jobless, wifeless, hopeless.

It was a sad and desolate place on a winter night, this
train station, dark and gray, almost Soviet in its concrete
utilitarian slabness. View from the elevated platform, looking south: parking lot, Sunrise Highway, clot of fast food
restaurants at the intersection, encrustation of low commercial buildings stretching out in either direction. Past them,
residential subdivisions like fields filled with crops of hous-
ing for the commutitariat.

I went down the stairs and headed away from the lights
of the station. The sound of traffic on Sunrise Highway was
soon a whisper fading behind me. The streets I walked
led past scrubby, winter-hard lawns, the suburban tundra,
a light or two on in each house set behind them. Block

after block, the only variation to my eye—habituated over decades to brightly lit city nights—was the shape and size of the SUVs parked in the driveways. The streets curved this way and that past the rows of slumbering homes, just enough to soften the planned grid and slow down the occasional car. I walked in the center of the street just as I had as a kid, when I'd wander these streets with friends, hoping to find someone older to buy us beer. Just as we had then, I moved to the sidewalk when the lights of a car appeared in front of me, or approaching from behind, threw my long, attenuated shadow ahead.

I expected the house I arrived at to be fully dark, but not only was every window bright with light, there were glaring floodlights on the roof illuminating the yards, front and back. My mother had the lights on a timer, it turned out, and she had never been given to understatement. Feeling like a prisoner breaking back in, imagining guards tracking me from behind the floodlights, I walked around to the back of the house, reached down into the mouth of the large and colorful Mexican-style ceramic frog squatting on the patio, retrieved the key, and let myself in.

From the kitchen, where I entered, I could see that nothing had changed since I'd last visited, for my mother's birthday, her seventy-eighth. The living room, where she entertained, displayed a distinct combination of unshakable kitsch roots and acquired aspirational overlay. At one end of a faux-Navajo-patterned couch was a table with a Tiffany-style lamp, a couple of fake Fabergé eggs nestled amid its feet. At the other end, a Doric pedestal of trompe l'oeil marble presented a large crystal swan, of which she was particularly proud. A glass-shelved bookcase against the wall displayed like trophies the bestsellers she had read with her book club.

A staircase led up to the bedrooms; another led down below deck, to the basement. I got a can of Fresca, with which the refrigerator was always stocked, and headed there, where my father, who had not lasted all that many years after begetting me, had established for himself a den. The beat-up couch he had sprawled on in his boxer shorts, drinking beer and scratching his balls, was still there, as was the bulky cathode-ray TV he'd watched whilst scratching them. Not far away was his pool table, its felt worn and faded. Through a door in a wall of cheap wood paneling was his workshop, almost untouched since he'd died, where the light of a bare hanging bulb showed a battered workbench, an impressive array of Sears Craftsman tools, and a repurposed tackle box holding screws and nails and bolts.

Hanging on the wall above were a couple of wooden plaques displaying midcentury working-man's humor. *TROUBLE IS A WIFE, A GIRLFRIEND, AND A NOTE AT THE BANK . . . ALL A MONTH LATE*, one said. The other was an elaborate cartoon chart of breast types: peaches and watermelons and bananas, water balloons and gumdrops, illustrated with figures scarcely better drawn than you'd find scratched into the paint in a stall of a gas-station men's room. As a preadolescent, I had studied it with fascination nonetheless. Also on the wall was a shelf holding souvenirs of Korea: a dented helmet, a rusted bayonet, his battered sidearm. I'd found them fascinating as well, and for a while, in junior high, around the time I first heard *Sergeant Pepper*, I'd worn his Eisenhower jacket to school above my bell-bottomed jeans.

After he'd died, I'd moved into the basement, and while most of the seventies youth signifiers I'd installed were gone, there was still a Grateful Dead poster hanging in a back corner, along with burn marks on the pool table from carelessly set-down roaches. The daybed I slept on was still there, and an old dresser containing some of my clothing, forgotten band T-shirts and non-courant denim, all now decidedly vintage.

My mother's late second husband, Morris, for whom she'd returned to the Jewish faith after years of perfunctory Catholicism, had taken over once I'd gone away to college, and the shelves I'd emptied as I transferred my books to my apartment in New York had gradually been filled with Morris's. There were history books covering all the popular periods—Egypt, Greece and Rome, medieval Europe, the American Civil War—interspersed with lurid paperbacks from the sixties and seventies: accounts of UFO abductions and reincarnation, cryptozoology and the Illuminati, *The Search for Bridey Murphy, Worlds in Collision,* and *Chariots of the Gods,* the stories that had once made up the modern arcana. Now, of course, it had all been through the pop-culture grinder many times over, had lost all its strangeness and intrigue, rendered as familiar and innocuous as Saturday morning cartoons.

Morris had also installed a heavy, industrial-gray metal desk, along with a now-outdated Dell desktop, from which he'd kept tabs on his large-appliances empire until he'd keeled over while sitting at it a final time. I pushed his old computer aside to make room for my laptop and opened it, but could not sit still. I was filled with an unpleasant claustrophobic energy, a simmering, directionless impulse to immediate action, like a prisoner still compelled to throw himself at the bars of his cage after the door has clanged unmistakably shut.

When you look back, it's easy to fall into the trap of seeing a story there, a story about your intentions and their consequences, with you at the helm. If that were really how things worked and not just a sort of apophenia, the decision I made then would have been trivial. Instead, it was the first step down a path that led me, I can now see, to the things that I would do; led me, inevitably, to murder.

I decided to go to the gym.

THERE WAS a twenty-four-hour gym a fifteen-minute walk away. As somebody who spent most of his time at a desk, I tried to work out every day. Resigned to an extended stay, I thought I would look into some sort of membership. Not the most practical thing I could be doing, but it would get me out of the house for a bit, give me a destination, an excuse to take a walk through the night and keep my mind off my wife, Sarah, when and if she might forgive me, and how I had—not to put too fine a point on it—fucked up.

The gym was in a nearby shopping center, at one end of a long row of storefronts—hardware store, Hallmark card shop, lawn and garden supply, H&R Block, etc., all of them dark now—in the building that had been the Seaford Cinema when I was a kid. As I walked across the parking lot toward the gym, wending my way through the array of cars fanned out around its entrance, the full-glass facade presented a diorama of ellipticals and treadmills, the people on them performing like a mechanical Christmas display in a Fifth Avenue department-store window.

Inside, I asked the smiling young trainer behind the reception desk about short-term memberships, and she bounded off to fetch a manager. I turned to look over the bright, cavernous space, and my eyes were immediately drawn to a woman halfway across the room, tightly sheathed in shiny fabric; from this angle she offered a pleasant combination of lithe curves and a just-noticeable bounce as she ran on her treadmill.

I do my best not to stare, to keep my male gaze holstered, but there is a default setting, and the default setting is to look; it can take a conscious act of will not to. This becomes harder when you have not been welcome in your wife's bed for some time, something, I should make clear, that was in no way Sarah's fault.

While my wife had been away on a book tour for her latest novel, I had strayed. At the time I told myself it was a justified act. Who knew what Sarah was up to while she was out of town and out of sight? I certainly would have been tempted if I'd been in her position and a fan had made herself available to me. Besides, I told myself at the time, it would in the end be *good* for us! I would be reclaiming some independence and dignity, restoring balance in a relationship that had steadily reduced me to the role of support staff. Again, though: not her fault.

Here is the thing. When Sarah had given me the first chapters of *Santa Country*, it was immediately obvious to me it was going to be better than anything I would ever write. I am a decent enough writer, and I might write any number of good books, but the market already has more than enough good books to keep everybody supplied with good books forever. Sarah's novel, though—and I can't overstate how clear this was to me from the start—was a work of genius. If I believed in the value of what I did for a living, writing and editing books, if that meant anything at all, then I had to acknowledge that her work was of far greater value than anything I was going to produce. So I assigned a lower priority to the beginnings of what I already suspected would be my third poorly received novel and focused on making sure Sarah didn't have to worry about money or housework or anything else.

I mean, what are you going to do?

"Hey, David Foster Wallace! Get your head out of the clouds and do the dishes!"

And it turned out that I was right. *Santa Country* was not just a critical success, it was hugely popular. It changed our lives. There was money, there was attention, and she bought a big, new townhouse for us to live in. There were also many occasions when Sarah was out of town doing publicity, and, well, I've already explained that, haven't I?

Now, here I was, exiled to the South Shore of Long Island, land of the obvious and the ordinary, a place of thwarted ambitions and tempered expectations, occupying myself by fantasizing about the bouncing—

"Roger? Roger Olivetti?"

I realized first that there was no longer anybody on the treadmill I had been unfocusedly staring at, and next that all that lithe bouncing had been Lisa Capitano, who was now approaching me.

When I was twenty-two, I'd enjoyed a series of assignations with Lisa, five years younger, a summer of making out in cars, nights on blankets at Jones Beach. I now had the disorienting experience of aligning my memory of that playful teenaged girl with the middle-aged woman standing before me. For all that, though, she looked good; if I hadn't known how old she was—forty-seven—I would have guessed she was ten years younger. She wasn't quite as sleek in her Lycra second skin as she had appeared from a distance, but she was still slim and curvy, with big, dark eyes, and black, expensively styled, shoulder-length hair, which was remarkably undisturbed, given that she'd just been running on a treadmill.

"Lisa," I said. "This is a surprise."

"I'm not sure why. I live here. You're the surprise, Roger."

Unsure of the etiquette—hug? cheek-press? handshake?— I settled for holding out my hand. She looked at it, amused, then took it in both of hers and leaned in, up on her toes, to kiss me on the cheek.

"What in the world are you doing here?" she asked, eyes wide, making it sound as if discovering me in the gym was the most unlikely and wondrous thing that had happened to her in years.

"Nothing much. I needed a break from the city. My mother's house is empty, so here I am."

"Oh, no!" she said. "I just saw her! Did she—I mean is she . . ."

"No! Not at all. Enjoying the high life in Florida. Healthy as a Jewish horse. I have no doubt she'll outlive me."

"Oh, that's a relief. I'd hate to think anything happened to that sweet old woman." She looked me up and down. "You look good."

"Thanks, and you—"

"How do I look?" she asked. "I've been trying to get back in shape. Do you think it's working?" She spun around to give me a full view of her progress.

"It's working remarkably well," I said, though I suspected she'd never been out of shape.

She beamed at me, put her hand on my chest, gave me a little push. "Are you flirting with me?"

"Do you want me to be flirting with you?"

She opened her mouth as if I'd said something outrageous, then said, "You are *so* funny, Roger!"

"Listen," I said, as she fished around in the bag she carried over her shoulder, "do you want to—"

"Yes, Roger, I do," she said, and held out a card to me. "Why don't you call me, and maybe we will."

I admit to being a little taken aback, at a momentary loss for a smooth response. Instead, I looked down at her card.

"Real estate? That can't be good right now."

"Oh, you'd be surprised. Lots of opportunities for a girl who knows what she's doing," she said, and smiled. "Call me, Roger." She leaned in to kiss me on the cheek again, then walked away toward the locker rooms, and it seemed like the walk of a woman who wanted you to watch.

Chapter Two

I should explain something before I go too much further. I've worked on hundreds of books, and I know that you don't generally get far with readers without giving them a sympathetic viewpoint character. While I'm not so foolish as to think that my actions will actually elicit sympathy, if I'm going to be that character, I should at least provide enough context to establish understanding, and from there, perhaps, among more generous readers, sympathy might grow. My goal here is not to convince anyone that I made good choices, just that, at the time that I made them, my choices were neither unreasonable nor particularly perverse. To the extent, of course, that any of us make any choices at all.

Now, I know this isn't something one normally talks about—it is in fact something one is actively discouraged from talking about—but for my story to make sense, I am going to have to mention that I am unusually good-looking.

I don't want to overstate this. I'm not one of those people who is so good-looking that it is in effect a superpower; voices don't hush when I walk into a room. But while I'm not movie-star handsome, I wouldn't be out of place as the movie star's less wholesome rival, the one he wins the girl away from. When I walk into a room, women tend to notice; they continue their conversations, but their eyes follow me,

16

and they're usually receptive when I say hello later. I started out with extra credit in the bank, is the thing. I've always been able to cut corners that someone shorter, fatter, less square-jawed, would be required to negotiate in full. The downside, of course, is that with age, I've had more to lose. I understand that this sounds vain, but if I'm vain, it's a vanity without pride; it is no more an achievement than the color of my hair (graying slightly, but still a rich, dark brown, and thick as ever) or the size of my feet (on the large side), but there it is, and it did not seem unusual to me when, a few nights after running into Lisa at the gym, I set out walking from my mother's house to meet her for dinner, nor did it occur to me that Lisa's reasons for getting together might be anything other than what they seemed.

My reasons, on the other hand, were plain, at least to me. Since I'd run into Lisa, I'd found myself drifting off into daydreams of when we were young, when my life was less complicated and most of it wasn't already behind me. Lisa—not as she was, but as she existed in my memory— embodied that time for me, and it felt like I was being offered an opportunity to revisit it. In contrast to my fraught relationship with Sarah, it felt like a chance to take a vacation from my life. Of course, I knew Lisa would have her own fraught and complicated history. She would no more be the same person she had been thirty years ago than I was, but if daydreams were logical and stuck to the facts, we'd all just get back to work.

THE VILLA Maria Restaurant and Lounge, where we'd decided to meet, was a family place; my parents had brought me here when I was a kid. Red tablecloths, Chianti-bottle candles. There were older couples at half a dozen tables, most of them not talking to each other as they ate their pic-catas and fra diavolos. A young couple at one table looked like they might be high school kids out on their first formal date together, playing grown-up. Or maybe they were thirty and had just sold their startup, and were here to celebrate their retirement. It's harder to judge age the further away you get.

Cold wind blew in with Lisa when she came through the door. She walked straight to me where I waited at the bar sipping a scotch, said "Hi!" and leaned in to give me a quick kiss on the cheek, bringing a cloud of floral perfume with her. She took off her long, fur-trimmed, camel hair coat and held it out to me. "Here. Get us a table while I go to the bathroom, and then we can talk about what it's like to be a famous writer. I have to tinkle," she said girlishly, and tinkled off toward the restrooms in back.

If this were another kind of book, a showily postmodern novel from twenty or thirty years ago, I might insert a footnote here, with a clever title like "A Note on the Type." Instead, I'll just explain that what Lisa had said to me actually sounded more like "He-ah. Get us a table while I go to the beah-throom, and then we can tawk about what it's like to be a famous writ-a."

Lisa's speech was characteristic of this part of Long Island, the result of parents who had brought their thick New York accents with them when they moved up in the world, from tenements and two-family houses in the boroughs to their own homes in the suburbs. But no matter where you go, theah you ah.

I was not a fan of the accent—I'd begun the work of losing mine as soon as I arrived at college and discovered I had one—but I had grown up with it, and unless I was listening critically, it didn't leap out at me, so I will skip any further tortured phonetic renderings.

"So," she said, after we were seated and she'd ordered a chocolate martini, "are you writing a new book? I want to hear all about it."

"I am, but I don't like to talk about them at this stage," I said, which was sort of true, or, if you were going to get technical, not true. It was more that I didn't want to talk about my third novel at all, the book I was nominally writing, because while I'd never entirely given up on it, I'd completely lost any momentum. It was right now an amorphous and disconnected assemblage of truncated openings and notes and outlines that I had continued to plug away at half-heartedly, without ever developing any sense of where it was headed or what shape it might assume. And since the series of crises that led to my new suburban lifestyle, I hadn't even been doing that, and was instead scrambling to keep money coming in. I was now occupied with editing *A Bewilderment of Echoes*, a 250,000-word novel that was going to be self-published on Amazon, a job I'd found on craigslist.

"Okay," Lisa said. "Then tell me what it's like to be a famous writer."

"If by famous writer you mean I published a couple of books, sure. Actual famous writers would laugh at that, though." This was neither rhetoric nor conjecture.

"Well, I don't know anybody else that published a novel, so you're a famous writer as far as I'm concerned."

"Good enough for me. That shall be my identity for the evening. Roger Olivetti, famous writer," I said in an orotund, self-mocking voice, but it was an identity I had once hoped to inhabit. At this late stage, of course, it had become vanishingly unlikely. My wife's application for the position, however, had been accepted. Sarah Scott, famous writer, no voice effects necessary.

Lisa laughed delightedly, reached out and touched my arm.

"You always were so clever," she said. "My mother was so proud when she saw your first novel. She ordered two copies and kept one on display on her desk. She told everyone to read it." Lisa's mother was a librarian, had worked at the library near my house. I'd known her since junior high, and first knew Lisa when she was a little kid playing behind her mother's desk while I checked out books.

"You know, I wouldn't mind saying hello to her while I'm out here," I said, and Lisa's mood abruptly fell.

"Oh, Roger, you wouldn't want to. It's so terrible now."

"What's wrong? Is she sick?"

"It's awful, Roger. She has dementia, and it keeps getting worse. Sometimes she doesn't even recognize me."

Until that moment, Mrs. Capitano had existed in the back of my mind as I'd last seen her: smart, vital, always ready to discuss what I'd been reading or recommend something new; probably younger then than I am now. I was thrown by the abrupt erasure of that image and its replacement with this new one. "That's terrible. I'm sorry to hear that."

"She's been in a nursing home for a while now. They take good care of her, but it's so expensive! Sometimes I don't know how I'm going to keep her there." She picked up her glass, found it empty, pouted her lips.

I waved the waiter over and ordered us another round. I thought about my friend Stacy, an editor at Penguin. She visited her mother's Upper East Side apartment most days after work, where the cost of round-the-clock home-health aides had drained her mother's savings and the life-insurance money from her father, and was now eating into what Stacy had managed to put away. She was regularly called away from meetings to rush to the hospital, where modern medicine managed to put her mother's death off a little while longer.

After a minute, I said, "If it ever looks like I'm going that way, I'll pull the plug myself."

"Really? You would do that?"

"Well, sure," I said. "If it got grim enough. I'm not going to go gentle into that good night, but I'm not much for raging to no purpose either. I choose Option C."

"What?" She looked lost.

"I'm saying I would want some control. It's a final way to exercise free will."

She stared at me for a few seconds, blinked a couple of times. "That was deep, Roger, but I was just asking if you really think it's okay to do that."

"Sorry," I said. "I do. I think it's okay, if you're suffering. And if I couldn't do it myself, I'd hope somebody would do it for me."

We looked at each other for a moment, then she put her arms around herself and shivered in an exaggerated way. "How did we ever get to talking about this? Let's talk about something else, okay?"

"Okay," I said. "What's your story? Do you like selling real estate? How did you get started?"

She brightened instantly. "Well, around ten years ago, we needed some extra money to send Kathy to college, so I took the exam, and it turned out I was pretty good at it. When Steven and I split up, I went full-time."

"What makes you good at it?"

"I know people, Roger, and I know a lot of the families around here. Nobody buys or sells a house because they're content with their life. Houses don't turn over because people are happy. The market around here, it's people buying or selling because things are looking bad, or they think they'll get better. Sometimes, nothing even really changes. You just have to know the right time to talk to them, and then give them a little push. That's what I'm good at, knowing when to give them that little push." She gave me a sly look, and for just a moment, she looked like the teenage girl who used to cut classes to run off and get high with me. "You want to know a secret, Roger? Sometimes it feels like if I gave someone a little push at just the right time, I could make them do anything." She laughed and took another sip of her drink.

"Wow. Maybe I should write a novel about you."

"I'm a pretty interesting person, Roger."

"I couldn't agree more."

We ordered another drink, then ordered dinner when the waiter brought them.

"So, what about you?" she said. "I heard a while ago that you were married."

"I'm not surprised. My mother probably went door to door to announce it."

"And everything's going okay?"

I lifted my eyebrows, gave her a pointedly sheepish look. "I'm here, aren't I?"

"We don't have to talk about that if you don't want to."

I would actually have appreciated the opportunity to talk it through with someone, but with the second drink, the evening was taking on a buzzy glow, and the more expansive and randy I felt, the more distant all that seemed. Besides, talking about cheating on my wife wasn't going to put me in the best of lights.

So we drank our drinks and ate our food and flirted a bit more, and managed to stick to inconsequential topics, nothing unpleasant or too close to home. Before I knew it, another hour had slipped by, and Lisa announced that she had to show a house in the morning.

She insisted on splitting the bill, for which I was silently grateful; until something changed, funds would be an increasingly pressing issue. I put it on a card and took her cash, and then we walked out to the parking lot. When we reached her car, she got in and I stood there holding the door, but before I could shut it for her, she glanced around at the nearly empty parking lot. "Did you walk here?"

"I did," I admitted. Not having a car on Long Island was highly inconvenient, and also faintly ridiculous, like you were the only person living on a Polynesian atoll who didn't have a boat.

"Get in, I'll drive you home."

It was tempting, but I could already see us parked in the driveway, making out in the car, first-date stuff, and I was trying not to alert the neighbors to the fact that I was pitching my tent at my mother's house. My mother was still as firmly a part of the local gossip network as ever, regularly catching me up on the doings of people I only dimly remembered or had never known. Someone might reach out to tell her there had been a car sitting in her driveway, and a strange man—or more alarmingly, her son—lurking about.

She would immediately uproot herself, I knew, and migrate prematurely north, where she would get permanently underfoot making sure I was looked after. Further, I did not look forward to her disappointment at hearing my marriage had failed, and even less to the advice she was sure to offer—she was an enthusiastic forwarder of multiply-nested emails and links to articles and inspirational stories about people who had either bounced back or kept plugging away, or simple, positive aphorisms misattributed variously to Oscar Wilde, Albert Einstein, or Marilyn Monroe.

"That's okay," I told Lisa. "It's not far, and I can use the exercise."

Your loss, her smile seemed to say as she pulled the door closed and started the car. "I know exactly how far it is. I was talking to your mother about selling just a few months ago."

"You were? She's selling the house?"

"Nope. That's a woman who is content with her life. Call me soon, okay?" she said, and drove off, both of us looking forward to next time, and, I assumed, for the same reason.

Chapter Three

Two weeks later, I was still waiting for responses to the dozen or so emails and phone calls I had out to editors I knew, asking for work: a manuscript to edit, a quick book-doctor job. Many of my contacts had aged out of their positions; others had disappeared in the waves of firings and layoffs since the recession hit publishing, their jobs eliminated, or filled by people in their twenties, willing to do the same work—while not as skillfully—for a half or a third as much. All of which I was aware of, but unexpectedly and disconcertingly, those who were still at their desks were not getting back to me.

Less unexpectedly, Sarah was also still not getting back to me. Emails asking for a chance to talk, an opportunity to explain again why she was overreacting and should reconsider, elicited no response, and my phone calls went straight to voicemail. She was hurt, I knew, and angry, which she had made abundantly clear before she finally came to the couch I had been sleeping on for weeks and asked me to move out. But Sarah had always been pragmatic, like me, and whatever problems we'd had in the past, we'd always talked things through calmly. I kept expecting some indication that she was ready, if not yet for me to move back in, at least to meet and talk about it, but that signal continued not to come.

I had, though, been on a few trips back into New York, for interviews outside of book publishing, new-media jobs I'd found listed under *Editor Wanted*. I won't bore you with the details of each specific disappointment; just imagine a quick montage here, scene after scene of me in a succession of big, airy, open spaces with couches instead of desks, gathering places instead of conference rooms, foosball tables instead of copiers, monkey bars the only thing missing, all of them occupied by startups and upstarts. Now imagine me the oldest person on the premises by twenty years; me being asked, not about my decades of editing and writing experience or the bestsellers I'd had a hand in producing, but about scalable platforms, about social media and followers and promotable content. Imagine me in a tie and jacket, surrounded by T-shirts and hoodies. Now imagine me imagining them making jokes about Social Security and the Gutenberg press as soon as I walked out the door, all of them laughing as they shouted, "Get off my lawn!" at one another.

I did not know the secret password and I was not welcome in their tree house.

Tail between my aging legs, I'd retreated to my mother's basement, where I'd made some headway on *A Bewilderment of Echoes*, which was about the love between a bold, independent young woman and a Minotaur, set in San Francisco in the days of the Great Fire. It was a type of job that had become common in the last five years or so, found in ads that popped up like mushrooms on mediabistro, Publishers Lunch, and craigslist: amateur writers looking for someone to clean up their novels before they send them out into the world, all of them certain they've written the one-in-a-million self-published novel that ends up a bestseller, when they had in fact written one of the 999,999 in a million that would not be read by anyone they did not know personally.

Most of these people knew nothing about how publishing worked, and many offered a percentage of the riches the novel was sure to bring in once it was edited for free. Others demanded that any prospective editor sign an NDA, a nondisclosure agreement, due to the widespread belief among amateur writers that New York City was full of nefarious editors perched in their aeries, making a fortune by "stealing their ideas." A few ads, though, were from savvier types, and Rebecca Jensen, a lawyer from New Jersey, was one of these. She'd agreed to pay me two thousand dollars, and though I would usually have gotten five thousand or more for a job like this, it wasn't nothing, and things were fast growing dire.

This was once again, I should point out, my own fault. Since the money from Sarah's book had started coming in a couple of years ago, I had been working less and less, letting her pick up the bills, take care of the heavy lifting, using my own savings for walking-around money. It had not been an issue. I had supported her for a stretch, and Sarah, ever reasonable, had not balked. Now that that arrangement had come to an abrupt end, I found myself running out of money and editing awful books, because *A Bewilderment of Echoes* was, not surprisingly, awful. One of the things you learn when you work in publishing is that perfectly pleasant and intelligent people can produce perfectly awful books. Nonetheless, I tried to give good weight, and had been hard at work imposing logic on the plot and grammar on the sentences. I had also lined up a couple of similar jobs for when I finished this one.

The other thing I'd been doing for the previous two weeks was having sex with Lisa. I won't go into a montage of these scenes, because, honestly, who wants to imagine people our age in bed? Even people our age don't particularly want to; fantasies tend to skew younger. Lisa was not, of course, the teenage sylph of my daydreams, but I will say this. In a sprawling family saga I once worked on, a Depression-era grandmother tells her brood, gathered around their threadbare table, "Enough is as good as a feast." This is a true bit of wisdom, and it has stuck with me. Women in middle age tend to worry that they are no longer sexy enough, but Lisa was still unmistakably female, with all the right parts, and she was appreciative and knowledgeable in bed. How much sexier did I need her to be? Any more would be wasted on me. My cup would almost certainly runneth over. If after all these years she was losing the fight with gravity, well, I was on the front lines of that battle too. And to be completely frank, with all the stress I'd been under lately, I can't say I had been presenting Lisa with lifetime-best performances, but she seemed pleased enough.

And while it is true that on paper we didn't have all that much in common, in practice it turned out to be a feature more than a bug. I had spent years cohabiting with an intelligent and talented woman who was my equal by any measure, and a challenge in more than a few. While Lisa was no substitute for the fully engaged intellectual companionship I had with Sarah, I found myself enjoying this other thing too. It had nothing to do with my marriage, did not intersect with it in any way.

I discovered that I was not immune to the pleasures of a more traditional relationship. I was, after all, someone who had been forged from the substrate of the mid-twentieth century. As enlightened as I'd since become, something inside me still found it refreshing, relaxing, to be deferred to; to know that we both understood who was smarter, who was in charge. Was Lisa really that fascinated by which contemporary authors I thought overrated and why? Maybe not, but I certainly enjoyed telling her, and unlike Sarah, she never interrupted to tell me why I was wrong, and then, even more annoyingly, go on to convince me that she was right. Yes, when Lisa laughed at my jokes it didn't necessarily mean that she understood them, or found them funny if she did, but the fact that she laughed nonetheless meant something too.

I had come to look forward to going out to dinner with her every few nights and then returning with her afterward to her house, where I could spend a little time not thinking about how I had, at fifty-two, ended up living in my mother's basement.

So, when I set out on Saturday night for the long walk to Lisa's place, after she'd said she wanted to cook dinner for me, I had no reason to think it wasn't something to look forward to, and I was in a good mood, feeling almost optimistic when I arrived.

Her house, in a development that would have been nearly indistinguishable from mine to someone who hadn't grown up here, was a low, spacious ranch, the porch light on above the front door.

"Why, thank you," she said, when she let me in and I offered her the cellophane-wrapped roses I'd spotted at a convenience store on the way over.

"Least I could do, with you making dinner for me."

"I'm actually enjoying it," she said with a little laugh as she led me back to the kitchen. She looked over her shoulder and smiled. "Can you imagine that? I guess I just like cooking for you, Roger."

In the kitchen, I hung my coat by the back door, and after Lisa handed me a glass of wine, I took a seat at the table in the dining room, separated from the large, open-plan kitchen only by decor and function. Lisa returned to the stove, continued what she'd been doing, singing along quietly to the nostalgia-inducing Joni Mitchell she had playing. She was wearing jeans and a little hooded sweater over a scoop-neck tee, and I watched her appreciatively as she turned things off and got out serving dishes and plates and silverware. With the music and the smell of the food, it all seemed terrifically appealing, in a traditional, mid-twenti-eth-century way. It suddenly occurred to me to wonder if that wasn't her intent.

Had she invited me here tonight to sell me this scenario? Did she want me to move in with her? It was fast, certainly, but it wouldn't be the first time a woman I was casually dating took it more seriously than I did. This time, though, maybe it wasn't a bad idea. As bad as living in my mother's basement was now, I was able to forget about it, get on with working or reading or spending time with Lisa. My mother would eventually be back, though, and hers was a very present presence, not easily ignored. I was still set on making it back to New York, but until then, moving in with Lisa was not a disagreeable prospect.

I poured more wine for us and helped carry the food out to the dining room table.

We were just sitting down to eat when a low moan came from elsewhere in the house. It wasn't loud, and I thought at first I'd imagined it, a trick of the music and the house's acoustics, but the smile fell from Lisa's face. Her shoulders slumped, and her face slackened, and for the first time since I'd encountered her in the gym, she looked her age.

"I'm sorry," she said, as she stood up. "I'll be right back."

She was gone perhaps five minutes and returned to the table looking sad and weary. "I'm sorry," she said, after she sat down. "I should have told you before you came over. I have my mother here for the weekend. They say it's good for her, so I bring her home every few weeks, but . . ."

"But what?"

"I just don't see the point, Roger. It's not like I can have a conversation with her. I can't tell if she even understands me. I have to feed her with a spoon sometimes. And, oh god, I have to clean her—"

I repressed a shudder, assumed an understanding look.

She stopped, gave her head a little shake, smiled deter-
minedly, and said, "You know what? Let's just eat."

"Okay," I said, and picked up my fork, "but if you want
to talk about it, it's okay. I don't mind. I can imagine what
you must be going through."

"That's so sweet of you, Roger, but I don't know what
there is to talk about. I feel awful saying it, but at this point,
I'm just waiting for it to be over. I don't even feel like I'm
living my own life anymore. I'm just going through the
motions and earning money to take care of her. Sometimes
I just want to give up."

I did my best to convey my sympathy, nodding with
her as she spoke, reaching out and covering her hand with
mine. It was possible, it occurred to me, that she was test-
ing me; that she wanted to see if I would still be interested
once I realized that moving in here would include this sort
of inconvenience from time to time. Honestly, I was going
to have to think that through, if it came to it.

"Well, if there's ever anything I can do, you can just
ask me."

"Thanks, Roger," she said, and smiled a real smile.

She had to get up once more before we finished dinner,
but after that her mother must have fallen asleep. Eventually, the table cleared and the dishes in the dishwasher, the
evening progressed to the bedroom, where we were thank-
fully uninterrupted. Afterward, as we lay together naked
in the dark, Lisa reached for a cigarette from the pack she
kept in the drawer of the bedside table. She offered me one,
as she had before. I hadn't smoked in twenty years, and
though it was never not tempting, I declined.

When the sobbing started in the next room, I felt Lisa
stiffen in my arms. She sighed and pulled away from me,
stood up from the bed and put on a robe she picked up
from a small armchair in the corner. When she came back
ten minutes later, she sat on the side of the bed looking

defeated, beaten down. I slid over and sat next to her, put my arm around her shoulders.

"Roger," she said in a small voice. "I'm a terrible person."

"What are you talking about? That's crazy. You're taking care of your mother. Anyone would be unhappy about it."

"No, it's not that. It's just . . . They send her home with so many pills. Sometimes I think about . . . giving her too many pills." Her voice got even quieter as she spoke; in the end she was barely audible. I didn't know what to say.

"Do you think I'm terrible?"

"No! I don't think you're terrible. I think you're brave. Most people are so afraid to be honest about these things that they'd pretend they weren't thinking about it, probably even to themselves." When she turned to look at me, I added, "I admire you for it."

"You don't think it would make me a horrible person?"

"Well, hold on. Are you really thinking about doing this? I thought we were just talking."

"I'm—I don't know, Roger. I'm so confused. I love her . . . I mean, she's my mother. I can't kill my mother."

I thought about it, thought about my own mother. As annoying as she could be, I would never want to do that. But, then, what if it would be a kindness to do it? What if that was the only way to end her suffering? Who else was going to do that for her?

Lisa's mother wasn't living what we meant when we talked about living a life. All the things that made up a life, made it worth living, the pleasures of sex, and friendship, and simple, physical well-being, were gone, and the intellectual pleasures had been taken from her as well. In a sense, she already wasn't living, and her death would be nothing but a formality, a gesture, a reification of a larger abstract truth.

I thought about it some more, and I'd be lying if I said it didn't occur to me, however glancingly, that it was possible

Lisa might be more likely to invite me to move in if she weren't dealing with this.

"I'm glad I'm not in your position, but I think you're just being realistic," I said at last. "If it were me, I hope that I would have the strength to do what was best for her."

"Oh, Roger," she said, leaning into me. "You've become such a good friend to me."

"I'm glad you feel that way, Lisa. But do you really want to do it? Are you saying that? Because if you do, we should talk about it some more. And no matter what you decide, I'll be here for you."

"Thank you, Roger. I'm so relieved I'm not alone with this. It's been so hard."

"I know," I said, and stroked her shoulder.

She lifted her face to me then, and I kissed her. Our breathing began to grow heavier, and I raised my hand to her breasts, and then she pulled back and said, "Only . . ."

"Huh?" My thoughts had moved on.

"Only . . . if I did that, they would know."

"They would know . . . ?"

"They could test her. They'd know I gave her too many pills."

"They might. That's true."

"But there's something else, Roger. I was thinking, it would be so easy if—but no, we couldn't. Never mind."

"What?"

"No, forget it." She leaned into me again.

"Lisa, I said I'm here for you. I'm not going to judge you. What is it?"

Her voice was almost a whisper. "You could do it."

"I could do what?" I asked, a little alarmed.

"You could just go in there and put a pillow over her face. It would be so fast, and it would be painless. You could do that for me, Roger."

"I could . . . *what*? Wait! Hold on!"

"You could, Roger. Remember you said you would want that for yourself, that you wouldn't want to go on like that? Didn't you mean it? She's suffering. Her life is over. You'd be doing such a good thing. It would be a blessing. I'd do it, but I just can't. She's my mother. But you could, Roger. You could do that for her."

"I don't know, Lisa." I really didn't. What she was saying was true. In theory, she was right. But she was asking me to kill somebody. Was it any different, though? If I thought it would be right for Lisa to do it, and I thought I should be willing to do it for my own mother, how could I say no to this? Wouldn't that make me a hypocrite? A coward? Is that what she would think?

"Roger, you know it's the right thing to do. You could do it for her. You could do it for me." She kissed me again, then looked up at me, her eyes big, and sad, and pleading.

"Will you, Roger? Will you do that for me?"

I DO not believe in an afterlife. I do not believe in a soul. All we have is this, here, a momentary window that opens into the world of the living. We poke our heads through, look around for fifty or seventy or a hundred years, and we're done. This is what I believe, and it makes life even more precious, I think, than it is for those who think there is more to it than that. What we do here is all that counts.

But that also means that nothing counts. There is no larger picture, no ultimate right and wrong, and while it's hard to argue with the assertion that killing another person is wrong, it's not all black and white.

I put on my clothes, because it seemed wrong to do it naked, and I brought a pillow with me so I wouldn't have to disturb her sleep by taking one from beneath her head. Lisa understandably stayed behind. The hall was dark, but the door was open, and the ambient light of the suburban

night coming in through the bedroom window was enough
for me to make out the old woman's frail figure on the bed.
I crossed the room quietly and looked down at her.

She lay on her back, still, her mouth gaping open. Her
breathing barely lifted the blanket that covered her. I didn't
recognize in the slack and withered features the smart,
lively woman who had talked with me about books when I
was young. A smell hung over the bed, the smell of medicine and age, a hint of corruption, of death, underneath it
all. I thought of all the reasons I shouldn't do this, and in
the end, there was only one: something inside of me said
it was wrong. I weighed that, some abstract moral princi-
ple, absorbed from a lifetime of soaking in society's values,
against the reasons that I should. I lowered the pillow to
her face.

Her struggles were brief and minor. He arms did not
even work free of the blanket.

I held the pillow down much longer than was necessary, possibly as long as ten minutes. Her spasms had long
since ceased when the light in the hall came on, and the
scene illuminated by that flash of light—the slight, still form
beneath the blanket, the bedside table with its medicines
and tissues—fixed in my memory like a crime-scene photo.

"Shut that off!" I said in a harsh whisper to Lisa's
shadow, now thrown across the bed.

When the room was dark again, I lifted the pillow up
and carried it with me back into Lisa's bedroom, where she
had retreated.

"Did you do it? Is it over?" Her voice was anxious,
strained, but also somehow excited.

I nodded and held the pillow out to her. She started to
reach for it, then balked, just looked at it. I looked at it too,
and then threw it aside, onto the floor in the corner of the
room. I sat down on the bed, and Lisa sat beside me.

"Oh, Roger! Thank you! Thank you so much." Lisa put her arms around me, leaned her head against my shoulder.

"Can I have a cigarette?" I asked.

She leapt to get me one, lit it for me, and I sat there smoking. A cigarette no longer seemed like such a big deal.

I DIDN'T want to spend the night, and Lisa didn't protest, but once back in my mother's basement, I couldn't sleep. My mind was, perhaps unavoidably, occupied with thoughts of what I had done. After several pots of coffee the next morning, I was tired and twitchy, and became obsessed, for about an hour, with the idea that Lisa would turn me in for killing her mother. It was ridiculous, of course. Nobody would believe I had randomly decided to kill the old woman on my own for no good reason, particularly when it was such a fortunate turn of events for Lisa. After Lisa called, solicitous and grateful, and sounding tearful in the aftermath, I put it out of my mind.

I didn't want to think about any of it, really. It had happened and now I wanted it to be nothing more than another thing I had done, like a book project that had gone south for one or another reason; an unpleasant incident, yes, not something I was proud of, but not something I had any reason to dwell on either. So, hidden in my mother's basement, I sent out more emails, made more phone calls, continued to scour websites for jobs. I still wasn't hearing back from anyone, including people I'd worked with and drank with, people I might have casually called friends. Even allowing for the dismal state of publishing these days, I could not understand it. Otherwise, I threw myself into my work, however slight and unrewarding it was, and moved slowly forward through the novel I was editing.

Thus, for long stretches of the day, I managed to forget the death of Mrs. Capitano. I suppose I should say the murder

of Mrs. Capitano, but I also suppose it should have crowded
out all other thoughts. It was, by some measures, the most
significant thing I'd ever done, even without assigning it a
moral value. Ending another life, surely that's bigger than
whatever small triumphs or setbacks my career had brought
me, or whatever relationships I had been in.

But that was not how it seemed to me. Every time my
mind drew me back to it, it seemed smaller, less radical and
abrupt. All I had done, really, was hurry her along. I had not
so much taken life from her as whatever dwindling number
of days she had left to live, and what kind of life had it been,
anyway?

Let's say, just for the sake of argument, that murder is
wrong, and has a wrongness value. Take a young, healthy,
happy person, who not only gets great joy and satisfaction
out of life, but is also a productive member of society. Call
the murder of that person wrong; call it, then, murder. Surely
that does not have the same wrongness value as taking what
could have been—and I realize I'm minimizing here, I'm not
deluding myself, but still, there's no denying it could have
been—only a few days at the end from a useless husk of a
person, who felt no joy or satisfaction, who brought no joy
to others, who, instead, simply drained resources and made
at least one person very unhappy.

Certainly, the second case could not be murder in the
same sense as the first. They were different in kind as well
as extent. Was I wrong to do it? It seemed to me that it
would have been wrong not to do it.

Still, it could creep up on me, raw, unadorned, the fact
of it, but rather than driving me in a Raskalnikovian direction, the more I thought about it, the more convinced I was
that it had been the right thing to do. By the third day I
was learning to look away when it presented itself to me;
by the fourth, I was ready to move on. Lisa and I had talked
every day, but only briefly. She had been busy with all the

arrangements that attend the death of a parent, and we had each been processing what happened in our own way. We gave each other the space to do so, but now that it was behind us, I thought, we could discuss anything this change in her circumstances might mean to us, to me.

I didn't go to the funeral, but I did want to show my face at the house afterward, when all the mourners converged, to give Lisa what support I could.

Chapter Four

I set out around one, about the time they'd be finishing things up at the cemetery and heading back to Lisa's house. I made it a point to stop in at a florist I had located online. I picked out an appropriate arrangement of somber yet handsome flowers, but had to do some quick mental calculations when the florist told me that they would cost close to eighty dollars. I had just missed a round of credit card payments, and if I didn't take care of that soon, the day was approaching when I would be coldly told that one or another card had been turned down. On the other hand, what was another eighty dollars of debt if I couldn't pay off what I already owed? I smiled at the florist and handed him a card.

The walk was pleasant enough, though the midday winter sunlight seemed sickly and phoned-in, making the neighborhoods I passed through look desolate—windows dark behind curtains and blinds, driveways empty on a weekday afternoon, lawns hard and spare—until I reached Lisa's block. There, cars were parked on both sides of the street in front of her house and those of her neighbors. The front door was unlocked and I let myself in.

The house was crowded enough that nobody took any immediate notice of me. To my right, the largish living room was occupied by small clumps of people standing around talking, clutching drinks, maybe a dozen all together, mostly men, dressed variously in ties and jackets, or more casually, like me, in khakis and a button-front shirt, open at the collar but tucked in. Against a wall, a drinks trolley with an array of bottles, a bucket of ice, and stacked plastic glasses. By the TV, a few kids were sitting on the floor looking up at something that might have been *SpongeBob* or *Dora*. A murmur of sound filled the room: the TV, turned low; the kids chattering; from the adults, quiet conversations, an occasional laugh or raised voice breaking through, abruptly cut off as the occasion was remembered.

I vaguely recognized a few faces in there, but Lisa's wasn't among them, so I followed the hallway back to her bedroom. I left my coat with the others on her bed, and returned to the front of the house to find her in the subdued atmosphere of the dining room. Five or six women were sitting at the dining room table quietly talking and drinking coffee. Not particularly engaged, apparently, as they all turned to look when I approached. Lisa stood up from the head of the table to greet me. She took my hand and kissed me politely on the cheek—she'd mentioned on the phone that she didn't think it would be appropriate to advertise anything just now—and I presented her with the flowers.

"How nice of you, Roger," she said, without much enthusiasm. I immediately saw that however costly a gesture it had seemed to me, for her it was another small task, and instantly regretted the purchase. There were two fuller, more expensive-looking flower arrangements in vases on the dining room table amid the cakes and boxes of bakery cookies, and two even larger arrangements sat on the floor against the wall, along with an actual wreath, at least three feet tall, with a banner across it, from a local real-estate association.

Lisa took my arm and turned me toward the inquisitive, upturned faces at the table, and for just a moment, out of nowhere, everything seemed to shift to another angle, and I was suddenly seized by the certainty that they all knew what I had done. But it passed just as quickly as Lisa began steering me along the table, reeling off a sequence of names that went right by me, until we came to a stop and she said, ". . . and this is Melanie." Lisa then excused herself to look in the kitchen for something to hold the flowers, and left me standing there, smiling politely, feeling out of place.

Melanie, who looked to be the youngest of them, not much older than thirty, pulled out the empty chair next to her and patted the seat. She was a pretty blonde with a shag haircut, wearing a dark dress, like the others, but the neck of hers dipped low, revealing the swell of her breasts and the twin bluebirds prominently tattooed upon them. "Why don't you come sit with me," she said, a welcoming smile on her face.

But just then, one of the children from the living room, four or five years old, came racing in, excited, calling out, "Mommy! Mommy!" She slowed as she approached the table, all eyes on her now, her exuberance drained by the dampening atmosphere of the room, or the memory of what one assumed would have been strongly conveyed instructions for behavior on this visit.

Melanie pushed her seat out from the table, said, "Come here, Abby," and the girl darted over and scrambled up onto her lap. With the table's attention on them, I took the opportunity to follow Lisa into the kitchen.

She stood at the sink, wiping dust off a vase, the water running. I came up behind her, close but not too close—we were in plain view of the klatch in the next room. "How are you holding up?" I asked her quietly.

She set the vase down to fill with water. "I miss her more than I ever expected."

"I know. I'm sorry. You made a hard decision—"

"Roger! Shhh," she said, glancing toward the women in the next room.

"Well, listen, I wanted you to know that I'm thinking about you all the time, and when things settle down—"

"Yes," she said, looking almost happy at that. "And there's something important I want to talk to you about." This was it, then. She was going to ask me to move in.

"Really?" I said, and while I cringed inwardly at the disingenuousness I heard in my own voice, it went right by her. "What's that?"

"Not now, Roger. I want to have this conversation privately." She smiled. "Do you want to come by later, after everyone's gone? Around eight?"

"Sure, that would be great." To me it felt as if setting the time to discuss it was the same as having discussed it, and, forgetting myself, I immediately leaned in to kiss her, to seal the deal, as it were. She turned a swift cheek to intercept me, and then turned to shut off the water in the sink.

"Okay. I'll see you then," she said, and left to join the others and get back to the serious work of mourning.

My business concluded, I saw no reason not to leave, so I retrieved my coat and was almost out the front door when I heard my name called.

Standing in front of the bay window in the living room, two middle-aged men were looking my way. One of them— solid, shaped like a barrel, big bullet head bald but for a horseshoe of densely curly hair, a broad smile on his broad face—was waving me over. I hadn't seen him in over thirty years, but his identity came to me quickly—Larry Petridis. We'd once been good enough friends that he had kept track of me and got in touch when my first novel came out. He'd kept up a fairly regular correspondence ever since.

"Larry," I said, stepping toward him and holding out my hand. "How are you?"

"Great to see you, Roger!" he said, shaking my hand with a great deal of spirit while clapping me heartily on the shoulder.

"Hey, Shakespeare," said the other guy.

"Steve, good to see you," I said, shaking his hand in turn.

Steve Campbell had been an apex jock in high school, lettering in all the high-status sports; you seldom saw him without a crew of jock cronies, teammates from football, wrestling, basketball. Steve's father was black, and Steve was obviously not white, one of the few kids who weren't, but nobody made a big deal of it, except for some lighthearted joking. In retrospect, though, it might not have seemed so lighthearted to him.

I'd played football freshman year and had been on the JV squad with him, but it was all too serious for me, and I quit after the first few games. We hadn't been close, but we had enough in common in drugs and rock concerts to hang out some, though our conversations never went much beyond "Got any drugs?" and "How are you getting to the concert?"

Still broad-shouldered and slim-waisted, he had the pronounced muscularity of somebody who lifted in a serious way, well past the age when most give it up. He gave my hand an excessive squeeze, which I bore with a grim smile. Steve was also Lisa's ex-husband.

"What are you doing here, man?" Larry asked. "You didn't come all the way out here just for a funeral, did you?"

"Yeah, dude, why are you at our house?" Steve said, then corrected himself. "Lisa's house, I mean."

"Just paying my respects. I was out here, ran into Lisa a couple of weeks ago, and when I heard about Mrs. Capitano, I thought I should stop in."

"It's terrible," Larry said. "Such a sweet old lady."

"Lisa's pretty relieved, you wanna know the truth," Steve said.

Larry ignored him, focused on me. "I didn't know you were here. You should have called me, Roger. I think about you living the high life in Manhattan all the time. I'm always saying I should meet some of your literary friends." He looked to Steve for confirmation.

"He says that," Steve acknowledged after a second, with a slight dip of his head.

"But, whatever, you're here now. How long you here for? We have to get together for a beer, talk about books. Life of the mind, you know? I fuckin' hate the unexamined life." He shook his head, a look of disgust on his face, presumably at the thought of those who embraced the unexamined life wholeheartedly.

"I don't know, Larry. I'm pretty busy, and I'm not sure how long I'll be around."

"Ah, come on. Don't be like that," he said. "Come over to the Galaxy! You know it's my place now, right? We'll hang out like we used to."

That actually called up a rush of nostalgia. The Galaxy was a diner on Sunrise Highway, a couple of towns over, one of a string of diners on the South Shore that Larry's father had owned, all with space-themed names: the Galaxy, the Comet, the Starlight. He started opening them in the sixties, in the Space Age, and thought the names brought him good luck. As I understood it, Lawrence Senior was a great believer in luck, once a brawny but savvy courier for some mob types, traveling from New York to Las Vegas and back, and they'd backed him when he'd decided to get into a more legitimate business. All the cash that flowed through the business he'd chosen probably hadn't hurt.

In high school, Larry and I would go to the Galaxy late at night, after being out drinking; we'd eat free and sit at the counter smoking cigarettes and drinking coffee, talking about all the places we were going to go and the great things we were going to do, and no doubt annoying the hell out of the lifer waitresses who had to put up with us. There were black-and-white photos on the wall behind the counter, of stocky figures in business suits and sunglasses, smiling and shaking hands in Manhattan nightclubs and Las Vegas casinos. These were the years of the *Godfather* movies, and I was not immune to the louche glamour of it all, of Lawrence Senior's ill-defined but distinctly shady dealings involving trucks of unspecified merchandise parked behind his diners late at night, and the self-assured, lupine associates who came out from the city to see him; of breezing in there with Larry as if we were part of all that.

"You know, I'd love to, Larry," I said. "I really gotta go now, but why don't you give me your number—"

"Nah, no need, I got your number," he said, and stepped forward, reaching up to grip my shoulder instead. "C'mon, I'll walk you to your car." He began steering me to the door, then stopped, turned to Steve. "Hey, I forgot. I need you to meet me at the Comet in an hour. Someone there you have to deal with."

"Sure thing," Steve said. "See you around, Roger."

As Larry and I stepped out onto the porch, I said, "Actually, I don't have a car out here. I'm just going to walk home, so I guess we can say good—"

"What? Don't be ridiculous. I'll drive you wherever you're going. Hold on, let me get my coat." He went back inside and returned in under a minute, then walked us across the lawn toward a sleek, black BMW, brushing aside my protests.

"Oh, just get in. I want to talk to you anyway. I've been working on something and I think this is really the one. I think it's my breakthrough book," he told me, which, if not exactly the last thing I'd want to hear him say, was in the top two or three.

"Oh, yeah? Tell me about it," I said, bowing to the inevitable, and getting into the car along with him.

I should pause here and share some history.

Larry had returned to Long Island after four years at SUNY Plattsburgh, where he'd studied hospitality and business administration. Over time he'd worked his way up to managing his father's empire of burgers, fries, and breakfast specials, and he did a good job; soon they were doing better than they ever had under his father. When Lawrence Senior finally retired to Florida, Larry started putting his own managers in place and decided that what he really wanted to do was write novels. He'd been following my career, and when he finished his first novel, he'd sent me the manuscript.

Unfortunately, Larry was one of those enthusiastic amateurs who was really meant to remain a reader. He was moved and excited by the thrillers he read, the Grishams and the Pattersons, but he had no insight into how they worked, why he enjoyed them so much. He lacked the ear to recognize the music that animates even the plainest of well-constructed sentences, and while he understood that certain words and phrases are associated with "fancy" writing, he had no idea how to use them, so he sprinkled them heedlessly onto his writing like multicolored jimmies over some terrible flavor of ice cream, like roast beef, or hair. His characters were always doffing said hat, laughing to no end, eating their respective lunch. When they weren't ensconced in their edifice, they rushed one-dimensionally through derivative plots that were somehow both entirely predictable and nonsensically byzantine.

On top of everything else, the novel Larry sent me was casually racist and revealed a crude misunderstanding of how the world worked. An underlying, matter-of-fact misogyny led to female characters who were either virgins or sluts, distinguished further only by the color of their hair and the size of their breasts, which were either large or larger.

I wrote back and told him politely that I'd enjoyed it. The next one he sent was no better, and was accompanied by a long screed about New York publishing, how he couldn't even get an agent to read his book. He asked if I would pass his new book along to my agent. Fortunately, I was on very good terms with my agent at the time and wrote up a respectful and considerate rejection letter that Darius was happy to sign and send out on his letterhead.

Larry was disappointed and asked if I could help him make his book more marketable, but that was not only a hopeless proposition, the prospect was nightmarish. I had deadlines looming, I explained to him, and while I'd like to help out an old friend, business is business, as I was sure he'd understand. Business is business, he conceded, but he continued to keep me apprised of developments in his writing career, sending me his further efforts, and eventually links to Amazon when he inevitably turned to self-publishing.

". . . so whadya think?" Larry was saying now. "It's just sitting there, and you can use it as long as you're out here."

I hadn't been paying attention as he'd talked me through the plot of his latest, throwing him *Oh*s and *Huh*s when it felt appropriate, and I'd missed it when he'd changed the subject. I quickly rewound, played back the part where he'd offered to lend me a car.

"That's really generous, Larry. Are you sure it's not an inconvenience?"

"Nah, like I said, I'm selling it. I can wait a few weeks. Glad to do you the favor. You want to go get it now? It's parked over behind the Galaxy."

It would certainly be helpful to have a car out here; I was tired of walking everywhere. However much I balked at the idea of accepting that large a favor from Larry and obligating myself, I quickly decided that the convenience outweighed my misgivings, even if it meant opening myself to reading another one of his novels. "Sure," I said, "if it's not any trouble."

As it turned out, it was more trouble than I could ever have imagined, but not for Larry.

"Great!" he said, and took the next right off Jerusalem Avenue to head up to Sunrise Highway.

"So, you see a lot of Steve?" I asked him, following up on something that had been worrying me.

"Yeah, he works for me. He's a good guy."

"Listen, I gotta tell you something. I've been, well, I'm sleeping with Lisa."

"Ha! You're still a dog! I should have known as soon as I saw you there. She's still pretty hot, isn't she?"

"Well, yeah, but the reason I'm mentioning it is, I was wondering, do you think she would have told Steve? Did he seem a little hostile? Like maybe he hasn't moved on?"

"Nah, that's just Steve. He can seem a little hostile. It's useful. In business, I mean. He's my right-hand man. The help I get these days? In the kitchen? All Mexican. Steve helps me manage them. Think those spics wouldn't steal me blind if they didn't know they'd be risking a few broken fingers? Me, I'm a nice guy. Sometimes that's not what you need."

I was silent for a moment, then asked, "He really does that?" sounding to myself a little naive.

"You know, from time to time," Larry said, without taking his eyes off the road. No big thing. "Occasionally."

I was a little shocked at Steve and Larry's management style, but mostly concerned about what this meant to me. "So you don't think he knows? About Lisa?"

"Well, who knows? Lisa's always been kind of a cunt. She might have told him about it just to fuck with him."

When I didn't say anything to that, Larry added, "Look, don't worry about it. If you think it's a problem, I can talk to him. He's a grown-up. He'll understand."

We pulled into the parking lot of the Galaxy, which in our day had looked a bit run-down. Now it was gorgeous, assuming you like that kind of thing, a perfectly re-created, streamlined art-deco diner, mid-century nostalgia at its finest, all chrome and glass and neon. Above it, a big rotating sign, red, yellow, and blue bulbs, inexplicably in the shape of Saturn.

"Nice," I said.

"Yeah, it is, right? You should see my newest place, in Syosset. Very classy. I have seven of these on the island now. My VC guys want to roll out a franchise." He pulled into a spot not far from the entrance, next to a silver panel truck with a bakery's logo painted on the side.

In front of the steps to the door was a harried-looking young man in suit pants and a half-tucked dress shirt. A folder sloppily stuffed with papers was slipping out from where he had it pinned against his side with his arm, and he was holding a clipboard with another sheaf of papers clamped to it. He was arguing with an older guy in baggy jeans and a gray uniform shirt.

"Come meet my son, Johnny," Larry said.

We got out and approached them, and when the delivery guy saw us, he turned immediately to Larry.

"Larry! Thank god you're here! I'm trying to explain—"

"It's okay. Don't worry, Rollo." Larry snatched the clipboard from Johnny and flicked quickly through a few of the sheets on top. "Ah. Got it. Do me a favor, Rollo. Go park around back and wait for me, okay? We'll get this sorted out."

"Sure, Larry," he said, and after a glance back at Johnny, accompanied by a dismissive shake of the head, he started back to his truck.

"Johnny!" Larry said, as soon as the guy was out of earshot. "How many times I gotta tell ya! Don't do this stuff out front! It's not professional. It upsets the customers. And stay on top of the invoices."

"I know, Dad, I was—"

Just then, a waitress in a neat little Mildred Pierce uniform popped her head out the door.

"Johnny! You gotta—oh, good, you're here, Larry. Someone has to talk to the guys in the kitchen about—"

"I'll be right in, hon. You tell them I'm coming."

When she'd gone back in, Larry turned back to his son.

"Things just get away from me, Dad," Johnny said. "I'm sorry."

"Ah, that's okay. You keep at it. You'll get it." Larry reached his hand around the back of the kid's neck, gave him an affectionate shake, and turned to me. "This guy is gonna run my business someday, Roger. Say hello to Mr. Olivetti, Johnny. He's an old friend. A big literary guy from the city."

I reached out and we shook hands, and then Larry sent him back inside, told him not to do anything else until he joined him.

"Come on," he said, and led me around the building to where a Volkswagen Beetle, bright lime green, waited. He snapped a key ring off a jangling assortment he pulled from his pocket.

"Wouldn't have seen you driving one of these," I said.

"Nah, I bought it for my daughter a few years ago. Just got her a new car, a Boxster. Never satisfied, that one. Hey, you know what I like to do? You can come with me. I go out to Jones Beach at night. No one's out there this time of year. I just park the car and look out at the ocean, think about the future, work out my plans. I got big plans, Roger."

"What, you mean for your next book?"

"Nah. I mean, sure, that too, but what I'm talking about— Why don't you just come with me, and I'll tell you all about it?"

"That would be great, Larry. Why don't we talk tomorrow, when I know what I'm going to be doing, and we can figure something out?"

"Good, but listen, one thing, don't take the car into the city, okay? I don't want to deal with cops and insurance and everything else if it gets stolen."

"You know, New York's nothing like that anymore," I told him. "It's like a theme park for tourists. New York Land."

"Yeah, yeah, whatever. Just don't, okay? I'm serious."

Like me, Larry had grown up with the near-apocalyptic landscape of sixties and seventies New York looming on our horizon, the New York City that had inspired *Escape from New York* and *The Warriors*. Unfortunately, a foray to the Lower East Side to score drugs senior year had resulted in an ugly mugging, and he'd never gotten over it; it seemed to have fixed that vision of the city permanently in his mind.

"Sure, Larry." I shrugged. "I was just saying." My phone rang then, and Larry waited while I pulled it out and looked at it. It was my mother; I let it go to voicemail. "Sorry," I said as I put the phone back in my pocket.

"Anyway, I have to go inside and take care of this stuff. We'll get together soon, right?"

"Sure, and really, thanks again."

When he was gone, I listened to the message.

"Roger, darling, I saw something on the internet last night—" I slipped the phone back into my pocket. She was always seeing something on the internet.

I unlocked the VW, lowered myself into the seat, and drove off.

CHAPTER FIVE

I was feeling rather pleased with myself as I arrived at Lisa's house and nosed the VW into the driveway behind her car. I'd debated it as being premature, but in the end, I'd packed my few things, cleaned the place up, and loaded my duffel bag and my backpack into the back seat; the alarm was set and the key deposited back in the ceramic frog. Maybe there would be some details to talk through, but I'd stayed overnight before; we'd work everything out. Counting my chickens, sure, but what was the harm? I had a car now, after all. If they didn't hatch, I thought, worst-case scenario, I could just take everything back to my mother's basement.

I was at the time still an amateur at imagining worst-case scenarios.

Lisa answered the door and pulled me immediately into her arms, kissed me thoroughly, even squeezed my ass in the middle of it, her mourning period apparently over. I returned the greeting, my enthusiasm ramping up quickly, and I broke off to take her hand and lead her back to the bedroom.

"No, not yet, Roger," she said, smiling, tugging me the other way, into the living room. "Come in here so we can talk first."

"Sure," I said, "but I think I know what you want to talk about."

She stopped, a puzzled look on her face.

"You know? How can you possibly know?"

"Well, it wasn't so hard to—" I stopped when I realized there was somebody sitting on the couch watching us, listening.

"Hello," said Melanie, the pretty blonde with the tattoos I'd seen there earlier that day.

"Roger, you remember Melanie?"

"Uh, sure. Hi, Melanie."

As she had earlier, Melanie patted the seat beside her, smiling up at me. "Here, sit with me," she said. I looked over at Lisa, who nodded and sat down in the chair across from us, as I took a seat on the couch.

"Lisa," I said, "don't you think this is something we should discuss by ourselves?"

"Don't worry, Roger. Melanie knows all about it."

I looked at Melanie, who smiled at me again, then back at Lisa. "I guess you two must be pretty good friends if you're discussing this with her?"

Lisa beamed at Melanie and said, "I do think of you as a friend, Melanie, and I hope you think of me as one, too, but"—she turned to me—"Melanie is a client. I'm going to handle the sale of her house."

I looked from one to the other, failed to make sense of it. "No offense, Melanie," I said, "but, Lisa, what does that have to do with me moving in with you?"

Lisa raised her hand to her open mouth. "Move in with me? You thought that's what I wanted to talk about?"

I suddenly felt very exposed and foolish.

"I, um—I just thought . . ."

"Roger, that's so sweet of you to want to move in with me, but I'm not ready for anything like that. I don't know how I made you think—I hope I didn't say anything . . ."

"No! No, all my fault," I said, my feelings—embarrassment, primarily, marbled with disappointment—no doubt visible on my face, which had grown immediately warm. "I'm sorry. I was obviously getting ahead of myself. It's only because . . . I'm very fond of you, Lisa." I glanced quickly over at Melanie, who was looking away from us, examining the wall, trying not to intrude.

Lisa reached out and took my hand. "I'm very fond of you too, Roger . . . maybe someday."

"I'm glad we got that sorted!" I said heartily, more than ready to move the conversation on to anything else. "What did you want to talk about, then?"

"Well! I had a brilliant idea, if I have to say so myself," Lisa said, obviously as eager as I was to change the subject. "Melanie and I were talking and . . . you know how I said that I'm good at my job, and sometimes people need a little push? There are so many people around here who would love to sell, now that the kids are gone, or buy a place in a better neighborhood, or move away, even. But the thing that's stopping them is, they have parents, parents who are sick like my mother was, and everything's still in their parents' name, all the money and the property. They're going to get it, eventually, everybody knows they are, but it's all tied up still. And so much gets wasted on the aides, and the nursing homes. It's just eating away at their inheritance. Sometimes, there's nothing left when it's finally over. And then what are they supposed to do?"

She looked at me as if I would have an answer for her, but all I wanted was for her to stop talking about this. I glanced over toward Melanie, who had been following along, nodding. She smiled at me.

"Lisa," I said, "do you think we should be discussing this here, in front of—"

"Don't worry," Melanie said, and reached over to put her hand on my arm. "Lisa told me what you did for her, Roger. I thought it was very brave of you."

I gaped at Lisa, yanked my arm from Melanie's touch. "You told her?"

Lisa nodded, smiling. "The thing is," she said, "Melanie wants to sell her house, and I want to sell it for her."

"Right," Melanie said. "The only problem is, it's not my house yet."

I started shaking my head, in part at how slow I'd been to understand. "No."

"You haven't even heard us out yet, Roger," Lisa said.

"*No*," I said, and stood up.

"Oh, come on, Roger," Lisa said. "It's not like you haven't done it before."

"That was different and you know it!"

"How do you know if you don't listen to us?"

"It doesn't matter. I'm not doing it."

I stalked out of the room, shocked and angry, determined to get away from them, from this conversation, but as I reached the front door, I felt a hand on my shoulder. I turned to see, not Lisa, but Melanie standing there. She leaned in to me, pressed herself against my arm, looked up at me. "Roger, please do this for me," she said, and I recognized the promise in her eyes. For a moment, I almost forgot what she wanted in exchange, but then I shook it off, turned, and opened the door.

"Roger, wait!" Lisa called from the living room. "I'll give you half my commission," she said as I stepped outside. "It'll be, like, eight thousand dollars!"

I slammed the door shut behind me.

I GOT in the VW and drove. I couldn't bear going back to my mother's basement just then, having thought that was behind me, and I had nowhere else to go, so I just drove, not blindly, but mindlessly. I let my ingrained memory of the area take charge while I turned things over and over in my head.

For the first time, I began to wonder how spontaneously the death of Mrs. Capitano had come about. Was it possible that Lisa had been planning that, manipulating me the whole time? I'd worked on a book that involved a similar killing, had done the research and knew it would look like natural causes to an EMT or doctor. But Lisa had assumed that too. How had she known? Had *she* researched it? Had she been planning this from the start? Had she been sleeping with me just to lead me to that act? I remembered the conversation we'd had about her mother, the first time we'd had dinner. Had she been feeling me out? And having her mother there that night . . .

As I thought, I wound my way through the gently curving streets in the dark, coming up to stop signs every few blocks, slowing down for groups of teenagers walking in the street. I wanted to slam on the gas, speed away from there, so I headed for the onramp to the Seaford Oyster Bay Expressway. I merged with the traffic whipping by at sixty-five, floored the VW, and though it took a minute for the little car to build up speed, I'd soon matched the pace of traffic, and was able to drive on autopilot again, so I could think.

What kind of person was Lisa? How could she do that to me?

Then I thought about Larry, his awful novels, his casual racism; about Steve, his violent, philistine henchman. I even thought about my mother and her awful taste, the tacky furnishings she surrounded herself with, the book-club best-sellers she read; about the simple answers to everything she found on the internet.

When I was growing up, I'd thought of the bridges and tunnels that connected the suburbs with Manhattan as a sort of a blood-brain barrier, a filter that only let you pass if you were smart enough. Getting to Manhattan was claiming your seat at the grown-up table. Those that stayed on Long Island belonged there, I'd thought; they weren't people to be taken seriously, and they were filtered out. I had never been one of them, even when I'd lived there, and no change in my circumstances could alter that essential fact.

As I thought about this, the difference I had always known existed between myself and these people, I made a connection that had escaped me before. Being around them normalized the way they thought, the way they lived. From a distance, in Manhattan, I had some perspective, could see them for what they were, but my ongoing association with Lisa, even the brief time I'd spent with Larry, had drawn me back into their world. It made me forget who I was, forget what was right, allowed me to do something I never would have otherwise done. Life really was smaller here, of less consequence. When you lived your life on such a scale, when breaking someone's fingers was all in a day's work, was it any wonder that life itself lost meaning? I had been involved in someone's death because that understanding of the world had seeped into me, infected me.

I realized then what I had to do. I took the exit for the Long Island Expressway, heading west, toward Manhattan. My home was there, with my wife. I would confront Sarah, refuse to leave until she saw that my place was by her side, that she had to forgive me, that we belonged together. My things were already packed, in the seat behind me; it was almost a sign. This was the right thing to do, and it was as good as done. Yes, I had given Larry my word, but what was it that I had promised him? That I would agree to his picture of the world, accept his values, go along with his racist fantasy of a dark and dangerous New York that no longer existed, if it had ever existed at all? No, I would not. I rejected all of it. I rejected them.

I drove on toward the city, dark shapes cruising alongside me, all of us carving our own tunnels of light into the darkness ahead.

Chapter Six

Sarah had first come to me by way of my agent, Darius Crovent. Darius had sold my first novel, *The Feeling I'm Not Feeling*, whereupon I immediately resigned from my position as an associate editor at Random House. My plan had been to live off the $15,000 advance—against the advice of friends and colleagues, as well as various busybodies: my mother; my girlfriend at the time; my dentist, Stewart Rosenblatt; a series of cabdrivers whose services I'd begun splurging on—until the arrival of the vast riches that were sure to come my way once the royalties started pouring in. The novel, however, was poorly received where it was received at all, and riches were not forthcoming. Last time I looked at my royalty statement, it had sold fewer than twelve hundred copies; at this rate, I should earn out my advance sometime in the mid-2040s.

While I was casting about for what to do next, checking the help wanteds and wondering if Random House still had a place for me, Darius came to me with a proposal. A celebrity memoir for which he'd gotten a considerable advance, and which the celebrity had made a lot of noise about writing himself, had come in a complete mess. If I could rewrite it quickly, and keep it to myself, I would prevent a great deal of embarrassment for everyone involved.

He offered me a generous amount of money, and I of course agreed. The book was a success and I soon stopped looking for work, because I became Darius's fixer, his on-call book doctor. I polished novels before he auctioned them, made the memoirs of public figures sound insightful and intelligent, or authentic and humble, as necessary. I developed a reputation, and agents and acquiring editors began steering their writers my way.

I would never get rich doing piecework like this, but I was doing okay, better than okay, really, and I would never have gotten rich in a ten-to-eight job at Random House either. It gave me a place to stand while I wrote another novel, purchased another ticket in the lottery. I liked not having to go to an office, having no responsibilities other than making people's books better than they were when they came to me, something I was very good at. When my second novel, *Cramming for the Turing Test*, came out, Darius let slip that it seemed to be the only thing I was good at. I did not have a counterargument. All I'll say about my second novel is that I hope it someday does as well as my first.

Sarah was one of the clients Darius asked me to work with. She was the opposite of somebody like Larry; she seemed to have been born hearing the music that made prose sing. But she also had something else. Writers like the author of *A Bewilderment of Echoes* were smart enough, and had an imagination, but were unable to make the reader see what they saw, to bridge the gap between minds, to make a story spring to life instead of remaining words on a page. Sarah knew how to do that magic too.

Darius had seen this in her beautifully written but static first novel, which had been her thesis project for her MFA. He might have sold it for ten or fifteen thousand dollars, and it would probably have gotten some good reviews, but Darius was sure that with my help it could do better.

I seldom meet any of my editing clients; I actively avoid it. It's almost never helpful, and it requires a different set of skills entirely. The real work takes place on the page, and can be accomplished emailing notes and revisions back and forth. Once I meet a client, though, someone who has entrusted me with their novel, the embodiment of their hopes and dreams, the repository, as often as not, of their self-worth, I become responsible for some degree of emotional support, and what begins as simple hand-holding can lead to me serving as both confessor and therapist. None of which I begrudge anyone, it's completely understandable and I've been there myself, but I don't get paid any more for all the time and energy it can take up.

Sarah, though, was special. Her novel told me that, and the evidence mounted with our first few email exchanges: she was intelligent and earnest, wry and charming, and all that came through even in our brief initial correspondence. After some quick googling, I suggested we meet, and over the next few months, sometimes by email, often on the phone, and occasionally sitting together in the back of a café, I showed Sarah how to move her story along, gently pushed her to make the plot more than a series of subtle, Jamesian shifts in understanding; how to make regular readers, not just aesthetes and literary mandarins, want to turn pages. Literature is a permeable beast; it can survive a pulpy twist or two.

Darius ended up getting her a respectable advance, and the book got respectable reviews, and I was pleased to find myself the one she called excitedly as each one appeared, and the one she turned to when it nonetheless became clear the book was not going to sell as well as we had all been hoping.

By then, Sarah was thirty-one. She'd spent her post-collegiate twenties burning through a sizable trust fund and had put the last of it into her MFA—against all odds, an investment that would pay off, but not quite yet.

Her second novel was as promising as the first, and we immediately got to work making it even better. This time, no money changed hands; it didn't feel right. I let her buy me a drink now and then, dinner once or twice. At the end of one of those evenings, things between us changed.

Sarah, I should mention, was lovely, and she carried herself with the grace and ease that comes from growing up with money. She was worldly in the way of someone who didn't hesitate to go to Berlin or Barcelona for a few months just because she felt like it, but she didn't know the working world, and more specifically, the publishing world. I was fifteen years older, but I'd published two novels, ghosted some bestsellers, and had a decent income. I also had a lot to teach her, and she'd been lapping it up. So, when she let me take her to my bed, it didn't seem unusual to me, and by never even glancing in the direction of its mouth, I was still riding that gift horse when the second novel came out. It got even better reviews than the first, but it still didn't sell well enough to earn out her advance. Her finances were getting tight when she showed me the first chapters of *Santa Country*, and as I've said, I recognized it instantly for what it was.

People say publishing is a crapshoot, that nobody knows anything, but it's just not true. For a writer of my talents, sure, a few of us get lucky and most of us don't. The third through seventh volumes of *Harry Potter* were not crapshoots, though. A scabrous tell-all by a sexually adventurous but previously private celebrity is not a crapshoot. Even a competently written entry in an established genre series is not a crapshoot; publishers know beforehand how many copies it will sell with a surprising degree of precision. Some things you just know, and everything I knew told me that *Santa Country* was not a crapshoot.

Still, publishing was going through some belt-tightening, and Sarah's track record made it unlikely that the fifty pages she'd written would get her the money she'd need to finish the book. I invited her to move into my rent-stabilized apartment with me; I would put aside my own novel, I said, and do everything I could to help her finish hers. Sometime after that—the book growing and getting better all the time—I asked her to marry me.

It was late morning and I was just back from the gym. Sarah was at the desk we'd set up for her in the bedroom, staring through the screen of her laptop at the world she'd created, the characters she'd brought to life. As was our habit, I'd picked up a latte for her on the way home, and I set it down beside her. As often as not, it would get cold before she noticed it was there, but that day I summoned her back.

"Sarah," I said. "I think we should get married."

I waited a minute—my words had a distance to travel before they reached her, I knew—and then she turned to me. "What?"

"I said we should get married."

She stared at me, brow furrowed. "Why?" she asked. I was prepared to say something about love, and what a good team we made, but I knew her well enough to recognize that she was asking herself more than she was asking me. I watched her think it through, consider the variables, weigh one thing against another. After a moment, she smiled at me and said, "Okay. That's fair." She turned her face up for a kiss, then reached out and gave my hand a squeeze. "Love you," she said. "You'll figure everything out?"

"Don't you want to plan . . ." I started to ask, but she'd turned back to her laptop and was already gone again. We were married at City Hall a few weeks later.

A year after *Santa Country* took its seemingly permanent place on the bestseller lists, Sarah's publisher flew her to

London to do publicity for the UK edition. At a book party a few days after she left, I ran into Stephanie, a chic, attractive, fortyish editor at Random House whom I'd known for years. We talked about Sarah's great success, of course, and after a couple of drinks, I'd confessed to the downside of becoming, in effect, the wife and helpmeet of a star; a WAG, as they'd put it in the *Daily Mail*. Stephanie had grown more sympathetic as she grew more tipsy and animated, and as the party wound down, we decided to continue the conversation at my place. We had a number of such conversations over the next few weeks. Sarah walked in on what would be the last of them.

I ARRIVED in our East Village neighborhood around ten. I was fairly lucky, and it didn't take long to find a parking spot on Tompkins Square Park, just east of A, only a few blocks away.

There was a cold mist hanging in the air, and rainbow auras glowed around streetlights, shifting as I walked past them toward the Tenth Street townhouse I had been living in with Sarah until a month ago. Even on a damp winter weeknight like this, there were scads of young people about, heading to and from bars and restaurants, to and from overpriced apartments shared by too many roommates or paid for by parents. Groups of young women, overdressed and underdressed at the same time, their laughter performative. Fratty clumps of bros, duding about, their conversation phatic.

Our home was on one of the few quiet blocks in the neighborhood. Both sides of the street were lined with dowdy but dignified brownstones, not a bar to be seen. In summer, treetops formed a canopied promenade from one end to the other. I still had my key, and let myself in. The first floor was empty, but I could hear voices coming from above me, male and female both. I climbed the stairs to the second floor, where the kitchen, dining room, and parlor were.

From the doorway of the parlor, I saw Darius Crovent, in his usual double-breasted suit, leaning against the fireplace mantel, surprise on his face at the sight of me; on the couch, Sarah, confused by my unexpected appearance, in an expensive- and antique-looking pale-blue dress, her long, strawberry-blonde hair worn down; and sitting next to her, looking at me as if she would prefer that I was anyone else—Freddy Kruger, say—still dressed in clothes from the office, Stephanie Crovent, my confidante from Random House. Did I mention she was married to Darius?

Darius was the first to gather his wits, and a wolfish smile spread over his face. "Roger, come in. You're just in time. We're celebrating."

I recognized that smile and it filled me with unease. It was the smile he got when he had maneuvered somebody into making a wildly inflated preemptive offer when nobody else had been lined up to bid.

I noticed then that they each held a champagne glass. An open bottle of Moët sat on the coffee table. Next to it, a fourth glass, full. Stephanie downed hers, and reached for the bottle to pour herself another.

"Hello, Sarah," I said. She looked at me, then away. I recognized that look too. It was a look I had gotten used to seeing recently: disappointment. Disappointment in me, and maybe in herself as well, for having trusted me all this time, for assuming she could depend on me to uphold my end of things.

"Do you want to know what we're celebrating?" Darius asked, walking toward me. Darius was an imposing man; he carried a good bit of extra weight beneath his double-breasted jacket, but he carried it like a nineteenth-century robber baron who'd just sent the Pinkertons to crush his striking workers. He put his arm around my shoulder and drew me into the room. "Yesterday I closed the film deal for *Santa Country*."

"That's great," I said to Sarah. "Congratulations."

"Thanks." She stood up, put down her drink.

"Sarah, do you think we can talk?" I asked her. "Privately?"

"Roger, buddy, sorry, but it's a bad time," Darius said, sounding not at all sorry, in fact cheerful. "We're about to go out for dinner. In fact, I want to tell you who—"

"Stop it, Darius," Sarah said sharply. She came over and took me by the arm, drew me away from Darius, and walked us back into the kitchen.

"Roger, this isn't a good time. Why are you here?"

"I'm sorry. You haven't been answering my calls, and I had to see you."

"Are you okay? Did something happen?" she asked, with genuine concern.

Something had happened, yes, a number of things, but I was not about to tell her about Melanie and Larry and Lisa Capitano's mother. Still, the concern in her voice gave me hope.

"No, it's not like that," I said. "I just . . . I love you, Sarah. I think we should try again. I know I can make you see—"

"Roger, I *really* can't do this right now. Can I call you? Where are you staying?"

"I'm, uh, out on Long Island," I said, which could conceivably have meant that I'd landed on my feet somewhere pleasant, and I could have stopped there, but I decided to get it out of the way. "At my mother's house. I'm staying in the basement."

She had the courtesy not to laugh outright at where my actions had led me, to refrain from gloating or showing pleasure at what must have appeared to her just deserts.

Instead, she gave me a smile of commiseration and said, "Oy."

"Oy, indeed," I said, which gave her permission to laugh. I joined her, somewhat sheepishly.

"Well, tell her I said hello."

Above our heads, there was a whoosh and a rattle of pipes as the toilet flushed.

"Listen, I have to tell you something," she said.

Heavy footsteps began descending the stairs.

"There are some pictures, and you're going to see them, if you haven't seen them already—*have* you seen them? Is that why you came?"

I had no idea what she was talking about. "No. What pictures?"

"Well, anyway, no matter what happened between us, I didn't want to hurt you, and—"

My phone rang, and Sarah stopped, waited for me to answer or not.

"Brad!" Darius called, out in the front room. "You missed the excitement!"

"*What* pictures?" I asked again, ignoring the phone.

"I've started seeing somebody," she said. "It was going to happen sometime, and I honestly wish—for your sake *and* mine—that it had been somebody else, and there weren't pictures of us all over the internet." She gave me a weak smile, took my arm, and said, "Come on. Let's get this over with."

I followed her back out to the parlor, where Brad Elliot, tall, manly, absurdly handsome movie star, stood drinking champagne. He'd been in war movies and cop shows, played good guys and bad guys, and in every one, he got the girl, although sometimes, having gotten her, he died, leaving the girl on the screen sobbing and the ones in the audience sniffling, damp of eye and crotch. He had sandy-blond hair, California hair, and his eyes were a startling blue. He was somewhere in his early thirties; his face was angled and lean, but boyish at the same time.

"Roger! Come meet Brad!" Darius said. "Brad's production company is making *Santa Country*! He's going to play Cameron. Isn't that great?"

Brad held out his hand and smiled the most winning smile I've ever seen in my life.

"How ya doin', hoss," he said in his friendly bass rumble, and despite everything, I found myself smiling back. The man was uncannily charming.

As I shook his hand, though, I couldn't help remembering that Brad Elliot was said to have the biggest dick in Hollywood, and there was ample pictorial evidence online, souvenir photos taken by various ex-girlfriends and fans with benefits. I released his hand quickly.

"Sarah's told me a lot about you, Roger," Brad said.

"Nothing bad, I hope," I said, finishing the exchange as required.

"Hey, bro, I'm known to be a pretty bad boy myself," he said, slapping a hand against my shoulder and laughing. Everyone in the room laughed politely, including me. "But, really, Sarah says you're quite the wordsmith, and she's quite the wordsmith, so she must know what she's talking about."

"Well, if Sarah says it, it must be true," I said. This time nobody in the room laughed politely.

"We should get going," Darius said, cutting off any further Wildean wit. "Already late for the reservation." Stephanie downed her drink and stood.

"I'm sorry, Roger," Sarah said. "Tonight just wasn't a good time to talk. You'll lock up when you go?" She walked over to Brad, took his arm, and they headed downstairs. Stephanie walked by, not meeting my eyes.

Darius waited until the rest of them were downstairs, then turned to look at me.

"One other thing before I go, Roger," he said, his wolfish grin returned. "You notice how ever since you fucked my wife, nobody will take your calls?"

I realized immediately—didn't understand how I'd managed not to see it before—why I wasn't hearing back from anyone, why I couldn't get any work. Darius had blacklisted me. He'd put out the word, and why would any editor cross Darius and risk not being offered the next bestseller? There was no percentage in it. I just wasn't worth it.

I tried to appear untroubled, take it in stride. "You know I'm sorry, right?"

"Don't worry about it. There's no need to apologize. Do you know why?"

"No, Darius. Why?"

"Because it's going to get worse."

I WALKED the three blocks back through what was now a cold, light rain and arrived at the spot where I'd parked to find nothing but a spray of shattered glass where the car had been. I looked up and down the street, tried to tell myself I had parked it somewhere else, but I knew I hadn't. I'd like to say that my first reaction was a sense of responsibility—that I felt bad for having taken Larry's car into the city when I said I wouldn't; that it had been stolen when I'd said that such things didn't happen anymore; that I'd let him down—but it wasn't. I was mostly pissed off that, against all reason, he'd been right and I was wrong. That feeling, though, was pushed aside when I remembered that my laptop had been in the car.

I began to head for the Ninth Precinct, over on Fifth Street, to report the car stolen, ignoring as best I could the knowledge that recovering my laptop was even less likely than recovering the car, and realized before I'd walked much more than a block that I did not know the license-plate number of the car; nor did I have the registration. I would have to call Larry and get all that information before I could report the crime. That set me to considering how he was going to respond. I was going to have to think of some way of explaining it to him before I called. So, instead of reporting the car stolen then and there, I decided to make my way back to my mother's basement and take care of it once I'd figured all that out.

I took out my phone to check the LIRR schedule and see when the next train back out to Long Island on the Babylon line was, and noticed the message light blinking. It was another voicemail from my mother. I pressed play.

"Darling? I'm home. I saw those pictures on the internet of Sarah with that Brad Elliot. Is it true? Did something happen with you two? I decided to come home in case you needed me." Her voice became a showy whisper, louder, if anything, than it had been before. "You know what they say about that Brad Elliot, don't you? Miriam showed me a picture. I didn't look, of course." Her voice returned to normal. "Do you want to come out and stay with me? Call me! I'm here for you!"

CHAPTER SEVEN

I awoke the next morning from a dream that Darius had gotten me a new ghostwriting client, a seven-foot penis. The penis and I were sitting in his office as Darius explained that for this particular deal, I had to pay the penis.

I'd gotten in after two A.M., my Babylonian exile resumed, having called my mother on the way to Penn Station and told her I was coming. I walked home from the train station in the rain and immediately changed out of my drenched clothes into MacArthur High School sweatpants and a somewhat tight Grateful Dead T-shirt I'd pulled from my boyhood dresser. Everything I'd brought with me from New York had been stolen along with my laptop.

My mother had been long asleep by the time I'd arrived, but now I could hear the thin sounds of morning TV—chirpy voices, laughter, applause—coming from the kitchen, along with the smell of bacon and coffee.

Something was nagging at me, something beyond the obvious. Then I remembered. *It's going to get worse*, Darius had said.

"Roger!" my mother called loudly from upstairs. "Are you up yet? I've made you a nice breakfast. Come eat before it gets cold."

The kitchen was bright, sun streaming in the large windows over the sink, the walls yellow where they weren't covered with the many commemorative plates my mother had collected over the years: all fifty states; all forty-four presidents (except for Nixon: "He wasn't a nice man, Roger. He didn't like the Jews."); assorted royals, including multiple Dianas; all nine of the collies that had played Lassie; and so on. My mother stood over the stove, cooking scrambled eggs and bacon for a party of four, and she now scooped it all onto a plate for me.

My mother, Ida Blonski Olivetti Faber, was a broad and solid woman; always tending toward heft, she'd given up the fight when Morris had died, and now gave the impression of a cushioned, ambulatory pillar. Under long shapeless dresses, she appeared to have a uniform circumference from bosom to knees. She was approaching eighty, but the added weight of recent years plumped out her face and gave her pink skin the aspect of a plastic baby doll's. I bent to kiss her cheek as she set my plate on the table.

I seldom consumed anything before noon but coffee, and when I did, it was a piece of fruit; this has been the case for almost forty years.

"Well, let me look at you!" She gripped my arms, looking me up and down. "You don't have any grown-up clothes?"

"It's a long story, Mom."

I got myself a mug of coffee from the counter and sat down; she sat across from me, where her coffee waited.

"So? What happened with Miss Fancypants Writer? She thought she was too good for you now, and had to get herself a movie star?" Sarah had not made a good impression on my mother, the few times they'd met. Too thin, too blonde, too young, too smart.

"It's complicated, Mom."

"Did you do something bad, Roger? I always told you you were going to get yourself in trouble with that little thingy of yours."

"Could we talk about something else, please?"

"Oh, sure. My son's marriage is breaking up all over the internet for the whole world to see and he wants to talk about something else. Could you at least tell me one thing?"

"What's that?"

"Did you meet Brad Elliot?"

"Actually, I did. Just last night. You'd like him, Mom. He seems like a nice guy."

She looked delighted. I noticed then a copy of *Eat, Pray, Love* on the kitchen table. I picked it up, and before she could ask me any follow-up questions about my wife's sex life, I asked, "Are you reading this?"

"Yes! I came up at the perfect time, darling. The book club is reading it again. It's been our book twice already. It's everybody's favorite. We eat the most delicious Italian food! Did I ever tell you what we call ourselves? We're The Ladies Who Read. Isn't that clever? Instead of The Ladies Who Lunch? Even though"—she stifled a laugh with her hand—"we always have lunch!"

"Yes, mom, you've told me. Listen, I was wondering, do you think I could borrow some money?"

Her usually pleasant expression fell from her face immediately. "You're having money problems too? Did you quit another job?"

"No, Mom, it's not like that. Things are just going to be complicated while I sort everything out, and it would be helpful . . ." My voice trailed off as she shook her head back and forth with mounting vehemence.

"I told you you should have gone to work for your father—"

"Morris wasn't my father, Mom."

"So disrespectful," she said, shaking her head again, but now shaking it sadly. "He loved you, Roger, like a *son*. He told me! But you pushed him away. And he was always trying to talk to you about *your* business, which I thought was very nice of him. You were always too busy, but he always wanted to."

"He just wanted me to help him get his novel published, Mom."

"Well, would that be such a sin? Have you even read it yet? It would be such a nice memorial for him if you could take care of getting it published now. How hard is it for you to talk to one of your publisher friends?"

After becoming Nassau County's large-appliance king, Morris had looked about for other worlds to conquer, and like Larry had decided that he was destined to be a famous novelist. After Morris died, my mother had given me a hard copy of his manuscript to read. I'd glanced at a few random pages, but now remembered nothing about it other than that it confirmed my expectations. At some point, it got bundled with the recycling, but she still asked me about it from time to time.

"It doesn't work like that, Mom. I'm a professional. I can't just pass along anything. It reflects on me."

"Well, Mr. Professional, maybe you should go write another one of your professional novels instead of asking me for money. And you know what else? If you'd talked to him more, and gone to work for him like I told you to, who do you think would have inherited Faber Appliances when he died?"

"You, Mom. He would have left the business to you, just like he did."

"Sure, but then I wouldn't have sold it, and I would have made sure you always had a nice job, and you wouldn't have to come to your mother, a grown man, asking for money."

"You're right, Mom. Never mind."

"No, no," she said. "If you need, I give." She went into the next room and came back with her grocery-bag-sized pocketbook and dug out an ancient change purse. She retrieved two ten-dollar bills and held them out to me. "Is twenty enough?"

I thought about explaining that what I needed was a couple of thousand, right now, to get a new laptop and buy some clothes, and then maybe another five or ten thousand, to start looking into a place to live. I wasn't ready to start thinking about what it was going to cost me to replace Larry's car if it wasn't covered by insurance. Instead, I smiled and said, "Thanks, Mom."

"Maybe I should call your cousin Mitchell for you," my mother said, and for a moment I thought she was encouraging me to spend some time with him, as she had often done when we were teens, because she thought Mitchell, a nose-to-the-grindstone type from birth, would be a good influence on me, but then I remembered that Mitchell had gone on to become a divorce lawyer.

"Thanks, Mom, but no. We're not getting divorced yet, and if we do, I won't need a lawyer."

"Of course you need a lawyer! She probably has some fancy Hollywood lawyer already. You'll see. She'll get everything."

"Everything's hers, Mom. She deserves it."

"Bite your tongue. You deserve too, for what she did to you."

While my mother could not help being partisan, Sarah and I both knew the money was hers, and I had no claim on it. If it came to that, I would sign whatever needed signing.

Besides, I couldn't afford my cousin Mitchell, and if we went to court, she probably *would* get a fancy Hollywood lawyer, who would tear Mitchell apart even if I could afford him. Or, say I persuaded Mitchell to take me on as a client for old times' sake, and he managed to wrest a piece of her *Santa Country* money away from her. It would not happen quickly, and while I needed money now, surely I will have worked something out by then. And when Mitchell proudly announced that he had won for me a percentage of the Bosnian translation rights, money I no longer needed, it would be no compensation for the way Sarah would look at me from then on.

"No, Mom. I'll take care of it."

"You always think you know best," she said, and sat back down. "So, eat."

I did what I could, but my body was having none of it; it was like trying to feed eggs to a tree.

"Oh, I heard something," she said.

"What's that?" I got up to refill my coffee.

"That nice Mrs. Capitano died. You know, the librarian. You know what she told me once? That you were her best reader ever. I still tell the girls about that."

I stood at the counter, suddenly shaken. I had managed to stop thinking about it, about what I'd done, and also about who I'd done it to. I hadn't wanted to think about who Mrs. Capitano had once been when I stood over her bed at Lisa's house, and had avoided thinking about it since, because it didn't change anything. Any sentimental attachment I felt for some past Mrs. Capitano didn't change what she had become. Now it rushed at me, though, maybe because my mother was there.

"Oh, don't be sad, Roger. It was her time. She had a good life. We all have to go sometime. Even me! Now, come back and sit down."

"No, I think I'll go downstairs for a bit."

"Have it your way. You always were so sensitive." Then she looked at my nearly untouched plate, the breakfast special for four arrayed on the table, and shook her head. "Maybe if you didn't waste so much food, you wouldn't need money from your mother."

I WENT downstairs, suddenly overwhelmed by the feeling that I'd made a horrible mistake, one that had set me on a path, unfamiliar and dangerous, that I was ill-equipped to walk. I sat down to think my way through it again, remind myself that I had resolved all this, when I noticed that the message light on my phone was blinking at me. There were notifications for two missed phone calls, and I'd received two voicemails. I also saw, when I looked at the screen, that I had left a number of browser tabs open last night.

On the way home from New York, wet, dejected, but unwilling to believe Sarah could be serious about Brad Elliot—he was charming, yes, and young, sure, and rich, obviously, and there was no denying he was very good looking, and fine, yes, he had a huge dick, but even in our brief encounter, I could see that he was not someone to be taken seriously; he was a buffoon, a very handsome clown—and set to googling him. Not, of course, to see pictures of his famous dick, though I couldn't help tripping over a few of those, but to see if there was any substance to the man, if he was in the long run any real competition. I had not given up on getting Sarah to take me back, and if Brad was the intellectual lightweight he appeared to be, I knew she would soon tire of him.

What I found confirmed my suspicions. He was one of those actors who believed that what he did for a living, pretending to be someone else, was something to be taken seriously, that his work was somehow important. "My craft," he called it in interview after interview, for one movie after another. Quotes from colleagues, about how he stayed in character throughout a shoot, and insisted on being addressed as his character even off set, were always couched in terms of respect, but it wasn't hard to read between the lines and sense the mockery that must have gone on behind his back.

He was also one of those showy Hollywood do-gooders, forever traveling to Africa to make sure children had clean water to drink, that their villages had proper sanitation and medical facilities. Sure, that's great, help kids, I'm not saying he shouldn't, but do we have to hear about it? Journalists just trying to do their job and file a story about his latest movie were subjected to endless self-righteous pronouncements about these vanity projects. I'm not denying that people are helped, obviously they are, but what is the *motivation* for all that help? Is it really to do good in the world? Or is it to be *the person* who did good in the world? He certainly didn't go out of his way to keep any of it a secret. Besides, the statements themselves were patchworks of sentimental cliché, and what's more, he could barely put two sentences together without using "based off" for "based on" or saying "infer" when he meant "imply."

I was looking through this material again, considering forwarding some of the links to Sarah, when my phone dinged an incoming email. Seconds later, there was another, and then another, and then still more, their frequency rapidly increasing, like popcorn in a microwave. When it stopped, I saw that they were all Google Alerts.

Years ago, when my second novel was published, I'd set up a Google Alert for my name. Given the reviews the book got, I was grateful when they stopped a few months later. Since then, I only received three or four a year, and none of them were of any significance.

This time, they were significant.

The first one was for an article in the *New York Observer*, a local paper that covered news and gossip in some of New York's glamour industries: real estate, show business, publishing. The piece consisted largely of an interview with Darius Crovent, in which he responded to an accusation that his client, Sarah Scott, had lifted key ideas for *Santa Country* from a self-published novel by an unknown author.

"I would stake my career and the reputation of the agency on the integrity of Sarah Scott," he was quoted as saying. "There is no possible way that she would ever knowingly plagiarize so much as a word from another writer. Anyone familiar with her body of work is aware that she is a completely original literary artist, and there is no mistaking the characteristic quality and the inventiveness of language in *Santa Country* for any other writer.

"However," he went on to say, "I have checked my records, and the novel in question was submitted to me five years ago. I never read it, but I did ask Roger Olivetti, who at the time was working for me, to look at it. Did he feed ideas he encountered in that manuscript to his wife, Sarah Scott, hoping she would produce a more commercial novel? I only know that Sarah Scott is a genius, concerned with nothing but writing the best possible book she could. Could she have been too trusting, too susceptible to manipulation by a much older, cynical hack looking to cash in on his wife's talent? That's not something I can know. I doubt Sarah could even say. The only one who knows for sure, Roger Olivetti, would have every reason to lie about it."

There was a link to the original article he was responding to, a post on *Gawker*, which was built around an anonymously leaked email from the self-published author to Darius, who I felt it was safe to assume had anonymously leaked it.

Other publishing and entertainment gossip sites had picked up the story, rewritten it, and posted it, knowing that a whiff of scandal associated with Sarah's name would yield a bounty of clicks, and the other Google Alerts led to the same story on *EW, Vulture, PW,* and the arts and gossip blogs of a dozen newspapers. Most of the articles managed to mention the movie deal as well, which allowed them to work in Brad Elliot's name and post pictures of Brad and Sarah.

I had no doubt that this would all eventually blow over, because it was untrue, for one thing, and unactionable for another—ideas are not copyrightable; if they were, the publishing industry would have been dying long before

Amazon had come along to kill it. Everyone is influenced by everything that passes before them, and even if you could prove where an idea originated, you couldn't stop people from working their variations on it.

Unfortunately, many amateur writers who were unfamiliar with how these things worked were preoccupied with the notion that somebody would steal their ideas. Furthermore, aspiring authors these days spent as much time following their favorite writers on Twitter and keeping up with the latest industry deals and scandals as they did writing. I was the latest industry scandal.

My phone dinged as two more emails came in, from the authors of the two novels I had lined up to work on after I finished the Minotaur book. They had each rethought things and decided to go with different editors. It took me only a moment to realize that the attention this was getting would drive these articles to the first page of Google anytime somebody searched on my name for years to come.

My plan for making a living during my exile from New York publishing, the lifeboat I'd scrambled into, hoping it would keep me afloat until I made my way back to shore, had been dashed against the rocks. Hanging in the sky above their jagged peaks was a big wolfish grin.

It had gotten worse.

THE FIRST voicemail was from Rebecca Jensen, the author of *A Bewilderment of Echoes*. I'd told her that I'd be done with her book that week, and it was now Friday. I was in fact very close to done, but the novel was on my laptop, and the backup was on a flash drive, and the flash drive was with my laptop.

The other message was from Larry, who said only that I should call. I felt a wash of guilt and dread, imagining the conversation in which I told him about his car. I was in no hurry to make that call, and instead rehearsed in my mind a conversation with Rebecca. The truth wouldn't do; it made me sound hapless and incompetent, which left me trying on explanations for why I needed more time without sounding like I was making excuses, which I was. Then, of course, I would still have to figure out how to finish the job.

Having gotten it somewhat straight in my head, I was about to call her when my phone beeped twice and flashed a low-battery warning at me; I was at 5 percent. It had been almost two days since I'd charged it, the charger was also in my backpack, and any chargers in my mother's house would be for her various Apple devices, useless with my phone.

While I wanted to put out the Minotaur brushfire quickly, I was relieved to have a reason to put the conversation off, and there was a Radio Shack not too far away where I could buy a charger. I went to my boyhood dresser, glad I'd managed to maintain a size thirty-two waist all these years, and abruptly learned the hard truth of vanity sizing. Of the pants I found, the only ones I could squeeze myself into were a pair of patch-covered, bell-bottomed jeans, variegated and clownish. My down coat, which I'd hung up to dry last night, was still wet, but an old hooded sweatshirt fit well enough if I didn't try to zip it up more than halfway.

I left my mother contentedly rereading *Eat, Pray, Love* and set out under gray winter skies in search of a cell-phone charger. I walked out of the neighborhood and headed west, past the storefronts of Jerusalem Avenue, more of them empty than I had previously noticed, FOR RENT signs hanging in some, others just dark. Wind whipped scraps of paper around my feet. The only trees I passed were weathered telephone poles, paper stapled to them, cheaply printed flyers for lawn care and handyman services, a row of telephone numbers hanging down from the bottom, some torn away, like a cartoon rendering of a bad set of teeth.

My hands were shoved deep in the pockets of my sweat-shirt, one of them holding my mother's twenty dollars. I was not yet completely broke, but I was glad to have it.

"Hey, nice pants!"

A battered white Chevy Camaro had pulled over and slowed down to pace me. I stepped over as it stopped and looked in the open window. Steve Campbell sat behind the wheel.

"Whataya, going to a costume party?" he asked.

"Ha," I said. "I look pretty stupid, right?"

Steve smiled and tilted his head in agreement. "Where ya goin'? I'll give ya a lift."

"That's all right. Just up to the Radio Shack on Hicks-ville Road."

"That's been closed for years. What do ya need?"

"A charger for my phone."

"Not an iPhone, is it?"

"No, Android. Samsung."

"I got some USB chargers lying around. You can have one."

"You sure?" I asked.

"Sure. Get in. It's cold."

It was, and he didn't seem particularly hostile. I had my concerns, but Steve had never been the duplicitous type. If he had a problem with me because of Lisa, he'd say so, or he'd jump out of the car with a baseball bat; either way, he wouldn't offer me a ride and a free cell phone charger. Besides, pedestrians can't be choosers.

"You comin' or what?" he asked, a bit impatiently, and turned the oldies station he'd been listening to back up.

I got in and Steve pulled out from the curb before I even had my seat belt on. As he zipped through traffic, taking quick glances over his shoulder and changing lanes con-stantly, he didn't bother making conversation, which was just as well, as we probably would have had to talk about how it was our music playing on the oldies station. In just a few minutes we were two or three towns over, in Merrick or Freeport. He turned into a development and wound through it to park in front of a large gray split-level in much need of a paint job and new siding; it looked like it had probably once been blue. There were a couple of sun-faded Big Wheels out front, and lying on its side in the driveway, a small, pink, girl's bike, colored streamers coming from its handlebars.

"You have kids?"

"Nah, it's not my house," he said and pointed to a window above the two-car garage next to it. "I rent an apartment from them." He took me around the back of the garage and up an exterior wooden staircase to a slightly warped metal door, a crack running through the glass window in the top part.

The room we entered was a low-ceilinged, all-purpose living space. There was a small kitchen area where we came in, the floor covered in old beige linoleum, peeling up at the edges. At the far end of the room, a couch, a coffee table, a TV on a stand across from them with speakers below, the floor there covered by worn brown carpeting. The lights were on, blinds down over the windows. An open doorway by the kitchen led to a bedroom; from behind a closed door within, I could hear a shower running.

Steve pulled open a drawer next to the sink. "Look in here. I'll be right back," he said. He hung his coat on the wall and stepped into the bedroom, where he knocked on the bathroom door, then opened it. "What are you still doing here?" he asked.

The shower abruptly shut off and a woman's voice answered. "Johnny screwed up the schedule again. I gotta do a double today, so I thought I'd better shower before I went in."

I half-listened to the conversation, audible through the wall, as I poked around among extension cords, batteries, and rubber bands, and came up with a USB wall-charger.

"Okay, but get dressed before you come out. Got someone with me."

"Maybe I won't." Laughter.

"You're funny," Steve said and then came back out, shutting the door behind him.

"This one okay?" I asked, holding it up.

"Yeah, whatever, just take it." He sat on the couch and began fiddling with a laptop on the coffee table. It occurred to me to wonder if he was planning to drive me back. It would be a long walk, and from the look of the sky, I'd probably end up getting rained on again.

"Hey, Steve, you think you could—"

He clicked a key on the laptop and a distinctive, off-center guitar riff filled the room, the sound a little fuzzy, the music hauntingly familiar.

He turned to me with a big smile. "Recognize this?"

I hadn't yet, but then Jerry Garcia's voice filled the room.

"'China Cat Sunflower,'" I said, and walked over to where Steve was sitting.

"Not just any 'China Cat Sunflower.' Our first Dead show. Found it online last year. Remember that night? We were tripping on the acid I got from those guys at Stony Brook?"

I did remember. It had been a great night. I walked over and sank down onto the couch next to him and we sat there together listening, remembering, as the band slid into "I Know You Rider."

"Hey, wanna get high?" Steve asked. He sat up and pulled an old cigar box out from under the couch, opened it, began rolling a joint.

"I don't know," I said. "I have a lot of things to do."

He paid no attention. He finished rolling, lit it, took a hit, then held it out to me just as Bob Weir sang the first words of "Jack Straw."

We can share the women, we can share the wine . . .

It seemed wrong not to.

I don't get high that often, but I enjoyed it when I did, and as the warm glow filled me, I put aside my various concerns for the first time in days. I was sitting there, nodding, my eyes closed, when I heard Steve say, "Call me later," and opened my eyes to see the woman who'd been in the shower headed for the door. "Bye," she said. She smiled at me, raised a hand in a hesitant wave, and left. She was young, around thirty, not quite pretty, but appealing; she looked a bit like a sexy, grown-up Cabbage Patch doll. I was glad to see Steve had found someone, and not solely in an unselfish way.

"That's your girlfriend?" I asked when the door had closed behind her.

"Whatever," he said. "Hey, do something for me?" He leaped up, went into the bedroom, returned a minute later, holding out a pen and a copy of *The Feeling I'm Not Feeling*, my first, underappreciated novel. "Sign it for me?"

I was gobsmacked, as the Brits would say.

"I didn't know you read that," I said. "I didn't even know—"

"What? That I knew how to read?" He shook his head, sat back down next to me. "Asshole."

"No! That you read novels! Sorry, but lots of people don't. It doesn't mean anything. And I never saw you with a book that wasn't for class the whole time I knew you."

"The guys from the team were always around. It wasn't cool. You know, I was always trying to fit in. I had a hard-enough time, just, you know . . . but I read a lot. Mostly science fiction back then. I tried to talk to you about books sometimes, but all you ever wanted to talk about was where to score drugs."

Feeling abashed, I signed the book "To an old friend," and settled back in to listen to music. I could see now in retrospect all the ways I'd misjudged him. I'd always thought of him as being like Larry or Lisa, somebody who accepted life on Long Island, someone who belonged here, but I now realized he had always been more like me. He'd once hoped for something better, a bigger life, something more than hustling for scraps in the suburbs.

Steve's father had been our PE teacher in high school, and had coached the MacArthur football team to a string of district championships. He was hard on the team, but on nobody more than Steve. It wasn't enough that Steve was the best athlete among us without even trying; his father always insisted he could do more. "Use your advantages, son!" I heard him tell Steve more than once. He pushed him relentlessly all through high school, and it paid off. Steve got a football scholarship to a Big Ten school, and looked like a sure NFL draft pick until his knee had been destroyed by an unfortunate tackle junior year. I'd heard about it from my mother at the time, but hadn't really thought about it since.

Now riding a wave of stoned, nostalgic camaraderie and contrite affection, I put thoughts of self-preservation aside and blurted out, "Steve, listen, I'm sorry, but I've been sleeping with your ex-wife."

He turned his half-lidded stare at me.

"Don't get upset, okay?" I said, thoughts of self-preservation returning.

"I'm not upset. I'm just a little surprised."

"Well, you had to know she was going to start sleeping with somebody. Looks like you've moved on too."

"No, that's not what I'm surprised about. I'm just surprised she's sleeping with somebody our age. Since we broke up, it's all been guys in their twenties, from what she tells me. She meets them online. They all want hot MILFs, she says. We had a big fight a while ago, she was on me about something, callin' me a pussy, and she wouldn't shut up about them. 'Three times a night,' she told me. 'They're like young stallions,' she said." He shook his head, got up, headed toward the kitchen, when his phone rang.

"Larry," he said when he answered, and returned to the laptop to shut off the music. "Nothing. Just sitting here with Roger."

. . .

"Sure, I can be there in twenty."

. . .

"Roger, he wants to talk to you." Steve held out the phone.

The pot had me stoned and relaxed, but now it allowed a moment of anxiety to turn into something else, something more like panic, and what could have been a chance to come clean about the car, tell him what had happened, slipped away. I took a breath, cleared my head, calmed myself as best as I could manage, and accepted the phone from Steve.

"Hey, Larry."

"You didn't get my message?"

"Sorry, I did, I was going to call, but my battery died and I lost my charger," I said, and immediately began to panic again, stoned enough to imagine he would somehow intuit from that the circumstances in which I'd lost it. He didn't, of course.

"You sound like my son. Well, listen, call me later, I want to talk to you. Maybe you can meet me out at Jones Beach tonight. And don't keep Steve any longer. I'm having some issues with a dishwasher."

WHEN STEVE dropped me off back at my mother's house, I found her in the kitchen, looking up recipes on her iPad.

I went downstairs to charge my phone and call Rebecca. I explained that I'd need a few more days, a week at most. She didn't seem bothered, which was a relief, and it was compounded by my near-certainty that she hadn't seen any of the articles about me, something I'm sure she would have mentioned.

Now I just needed a computer to edit her novel again. I'd remember most of the changes I'd made, and could do it much more quickly this time, but without a computer to do it on, I couldn't even get started. Against my will, my mind turned to the eight thousand dollars Lisa had offered me, and it occurred to me then that it would be easier with a complete stranger than a woman I'd known since I'd been a kid. As I thought about it, I realized that there was even a sense in which it would be less wrong. I know that sounds like a bit of a stretch, but if we're being completely honest, don't we all put a higher value on the lives of those who are closest to us? Don't we all walk by homeless strangers in the street who might die in the cold of winter without giving them a thought, while we devote our time, effort, and money to making those we care about just a little bit happier? Wouldn't we risk our own lives for somebody we loved? Yet we sleep peacefully despite the knowledge that children are at that moment suffering horribly and dying all over the world.

There was a time when the world was built on this idea, when nobody questioned that family, tribe, clan, country were all that mattered. It's probably built-in—every animal is programmed to protect the future of its own genes, at the expense of any creature that didn't share them. Many of our society's unquestioned values—protect the children; family is the most important thing—were obviously ex post facto intellectualizations of the same instincts that guided snakes and weasels, so why not this? Wasn't this at the bottom of all our values? Was it so much of a leap, then, to say that at the deepest level a stranger's life was in some way ultimately worth less?

And in the end, if I took all self-interest out of it, and Melanie's mother was in the same condition Lisa's had been, it would be a *good* thing I was doing, not a bad thing! I had put an end to Mrs. Capitano's suffering; I had freed Lisa from an unnecessary burden. Wouldn't it actually be wrong not to do the same thing for somebody else? Wouldn't the truly altruistic thing be to extend that kindness to somebody I didn't care about?

I was considering that, approaching the idea and backing away again, when I realized that I had been sitting there looking at a computer the entire time. Morris's old Dell desktop was right in front of me. It might be old, but it would have Office on it, and I could edit Rebecca's book.

I put Melanie and Lisa out of my mind and checked to see if it was plugged in, then powered it on. Before I'd lost my laptop, I'd been borrowing a neighbor's open wireless signal—thank you, belkin99z87r3—but a desktop this old would not have wireless built in. While it began to hum, the hard drive whirring up to speed, I ran upstairs, where my mother was eating a bowl of soup in the kitchen.

"Good, I made some soup for you. It's on the stove."

"Mom, do you have internet here?"

"What, you think I'm old-fashioned? Of course I have internet. They put the internet in my iPad when I bought it. It's also in my iPhone!"

"No, broadband. Cable, or DSL. Does the house have an internet connection?"

"I don't know. Your father took care of all of that."

"Morris wasn't my father, Mom."

"Well maybe if you talked to him once in a while when he was still alive you'd know if there was an internet cable broadband in the house."

"Okay, Mom. Thanks," I said.

"You don't want soup?"

"Not right now."

Downstairs, the computer was ready, a Windows XP screen waiting. Right-hand corner of the task bar, a pop-up. *Local Area Network Disconnected.*

I got on my knees under the desk, poked at the tangle of adapters and wires plugged into an old, sharp-cornered, metal power strip, and found an ethernet cable resting among them. I swung the computer around and plugged it into the back. Seconds later, the pop-up changed. *Local Area Network Connected.*

I signed in to Gmail, deleted another dozen Google Alerts, and downloaded a new copy of Rebecca's manuscript file to the desktop.

A few hours later, I was almost a hundred pages in. I wasn't doing as thorough a job as I had the first time, but, I told myself, nobody was ever going to read the book anyway. I added a few comments praising this and that to make up for it.

I was deep in the world of turn-of-the-century San Francisco, wondering how much the story would suffer if I deleted a particular coupling instead of putting in the time to make it sound less as if the heroine had three arms and the ability to turn her head completely around, when my recharged phone summoned me back.

"Larry, hi, sorry I didn't get back to you. I smoked a little pot with Steve, and it completely slipped my mind."

"I was wondering."

"Well, what's up?"

"Here's the thing, Rog. I was thinking that as long as you're out here, maybe you'd have time to help me with my writing. We could go out to the beach tonight, kick things around, then maybe have dinner after, and you can look at the new novel."

"I'd like to, Larry, I really would, but you wouldn't believe the situation I've gotten myself into. You don't need to know the details, but I've got this deadline bearing down on me, and I'm going to be really busy for the next few days."

"Ah, well. Business is business, right?"

"Right, Larry. I knew you'd understand. Okay, good talking to you. And thanks again for the car," I added.

"Oh, yeah, meant to ask. Steve said he picked you up walking up to Hicksville Road. Don't you like the car?"

I froze for just a second, considered confessing, but instead said, "No, just wanted a little exercise. Fresh air."

"I see. Okay, then. Go take care of business," he said, and hung up.

CHAPTER EIGHT

The next day, coming up on eighty thousand words, having stayed up most of the night to do it, my mother came to the door at the head of the stairs.

"Roger!"

"I'll eat later, Mom. I'm working."

"Roger! Your friend is here for you. Don't be rude."

Steve was standing in the living room, my mother hovering nearby as he serially declined tea, coffee, a nice piece of fruit, a sandwich, etc.

"Hey, man," Steve said. "Larry wants to see you."

"Why didn't he just call me? I told him yesterday, I'm busy. Sorry you had to come all the way over here, but I gotta finish this job I'm doing before I do anything else."

"I had to come here anyway. Larry wanted me to cruise by and look for his Beetle. Make sure it was okay."

I froze.

"Beetle?" my mother said. "What beetle? There's a beetle?"

"No, it's fine, it's, uh, in the—"

Steve raised a hand, cut me off. "Stop. Your mother was just telling me how the nice man from the driving service delivered her Caddie yesterday, all the way from Florida. It's in the garage."

"I wasn't going to say . . ." But I was.

"So, listen, Larry's waiting for us at the Comet."

THE COMET was located in Baldwin, on a busy stretch of Sunrise Highway, between a Best Buy and Empire Carpets, which had big, orange Going Out Of Business signs displayed in the windows. The diner's parking lot was full, so Steve parked his Camaro next door, in the carpet store's empty lot. Spare winter weeds grew out of cracks in the faded white lines; bits of broken glass shifted beneath our feet as we walked.

The Comet was identical to the Galaxy, sleek and shiny, standing out amid the depressed and worn-down businesses that surrounded it like a misplaced shard of some alternate, more prosperous retro-future. The window booths were all occupied, groups of diners talking, eating, waving their arms in the air to attract the attention of the harried waitstaff. The counter was full, lone diners sitting on stools shoulder to shoulder, variously attired in blue Best Buy shirts or cheap-looking suit jackets, hunched over their plates, burger in one hand, smartphone in the other.

The hostess, who was the woman I had seen in Steve's apartment the day before, looked surprised to see us, but Steve said, "Not now, Nicolle," and led me past her through the bustle of the place to a booth in the back corner near the restrooms, where Larry sat alone, his big solid belly wedged in behind the table, invoices spread out in front of him, his phone sitting atop a pile of them, a calculator on its face, reading glasses on his own.

Steve motioned me into the seat opposite Larry, slid in next to me. I moved over until my shoulder was pressed up against the wall, Steve's muscular bulk forming another wall on my other side.

Larry looked up at me, raised his glasses so they sat on top of his bald head. He did not smile.

"Larry, I was gonna call you to explain—"

"Shut up. Where's my car?"

"That's what I was going to explain."

"So explain."

"Listen, I'm really sorry, but it was an emergency, and I had to get into the city in a hurry, and, look, I don't know how it happened, it's a perfectly safe neighborhood, but—"

"You took my car into the city?"

"That's what I'm saying. But it was unavoidable, I had to—"

"What did I tell you not to do?" he asked me, and then he abruptly reached across the table and smacked me on the side of my head with the flat of his hand.

"Hey! You don't have to—"

He did it again. I looked to Steve, hoping for some support, but he'd picked up the thick, plastic-coated menu from the table behind us, and was slowly paging through it, seemingly unaware that anything untoward had occurred.

"What did I tell you not to do?" Larry repeated.

"Drive your car into the city."

"And what did you do?"

"I drove your car into the city," I said, mumbling like a sullen teenager.

"And what did I tell you would happen?"

"You were afraid it would get stolen, Larry. Look, I'm sorry—"

Smack. "Shut up."

I shut up.

He slid his glasses back down onto his face, picked up his phone, did some math on the calculator.

"Tell you what, Roger. Blue Book says twelve thousand for the car. I'm gonna give you 20 percent off, because we've known each other a long time. You owe me ninety-six hundred dollars."

"Wait, but the insurance! Aren't you going to get—"

Smack. "That's my business. You owe me ninety-six hundred dollars."

My mind flashed through possibilities, but there were none, unless . . .

"Larry, I don't have it right now, but how about this? You wanted me to look at your novel. I get ten thousand to do a serious job like that. What if I—"

"Nah. I've been reading some things about you online. I don't think I can trust you not to steal my ideas."

I slumped back in my seat. "It's going to take me a while to get the money together."

"That's okay. You're not going anywhere."

"Yeah, okay," I said. "I'll get it."

"I know you will, Roger. Steve, take him in back."

"What?" My voice was embarrassingly high-pitched.

"Roger, c'mon. You know how important reputation is. I can't have anyone thinking you took advantage of me and I just let you walk away. Business is business, right?"

"Wait, hold on! Nobody's ever going to know unless you tell them! I'm not gonna tell anybody!" While I was presenting my argument, which was airtight as far as I was concerned, Steve had stood up. He took me firmly by the arm as I sputtered on, and gently guided me out of the booth. I looked over my shoulder, toward the door at the front of the diner.

"Don't even try it," Steve said. "My knees are fucked, and if I have to chase you, I'm gonna be mad too."

"I'll be right in, guys," Larry said, and turned back to his papers. Steve led me past the restrooms and into a storage area, long shelves filled with nonperishables, five-gallon cans of blueberry filling and maple syrup, boxes of glasses, plates, utensils. The bare twirl of a compact fluorescent bulb lit the room. In a corner, mops and brooms, a dented, tarnished metal bucket on wheels, jugs of industrial-strength cleaners.

We waited, the two of us, Steve looking at me with some sympathy, I thought.

"Idiot," he said, shaking his head, but not unsympathetically.

I thought of Jack Reacher, what he would have done in a situation like this. Sure, Steve was big, but I am not small. I'm probably quicker and, I'd like to think, smarter. Jack Reacher would come up with a plan, a precise plan, based on knowledge of psychology, and physics, and the exact points of the body to strike for maximum effect. I considered my options and concluded that Reacher's plan would have started with not living in his mother's basement.

More than that, though, Reacher didn't hesitate to hurt someone who stood in his way, and while I have been in a few dustups in my life, I've done my best to avoid them, and I've never thrown a punch first. This was now undeniably a self-defense situation, but I had no desire to hit Steve. Reacher might have killed or disabled him with his first blow, a punch to the throat, say, or something involving a mop handle, but even in self-defense that seemed a little extreme. Steve was in the end a decent guy, and if his livelihood required him to do things that were questionable, whose hadn't?

I considered instead hurling myself at Larry when he entered the room, but was it really even Larry's fault that I was in this situation? Sure, he was unpleasant, and brutish, and wrote awful prose, and maybe he even—

The door opened, and Larry walked in.

"Give Steve your hand, Roger."

My planning was entirely derailed. "Come on, Larry, wait! You don't have to—"

"Give Steve your hand."

"You can't do this! I have to type! How am I going to make a living? How am I going to get your money?"

Larry considered it, looked down, brow furrowed, then looked up at me and smiled.

"Okay," he said. "Take off your shoe."

STEVE PULLED up in front of my mother's house, started to get out of the Camaro, then stopped. He reached across me and opened the glove compartment, dug around, pulled out an orange pharmacy vial. "There's some codeine left in here. It'll help."

He got out, came around, opened my door. "Come on." He helped me out, grabbed my shoe from the floor, then let me put my arm over his shoulder so I could hop to the front door.

My mother answered the door when he knocked, looked shocked at the sight of me hopping over the threshold.

"Here, Mrs. Olivetti," Steve said, and handed her my shoe. "You should make an icepack for Roger. He hurt his foot."

After some panicked clucking, my mother rushed off into the kitchen.

"Hey, no hard feelings, I hope. Just doing my job, man," Steve said, and left me propped against the wall.

"MOM, I need to have a talk with you about money."

"Do you need a little more?" my mother asked. She was sitting on the couch in the living room, in her favorite spot next to her crystal swan, her book open on her lap, reading glasses low on her nose, eating raisins from a little red box, one at a time. She put her book aside, sat up straighter, craned her neck looking around. "Where's my purse?"

"No, a serious talk about serious money." I hopped over, sat down beside her.

"You won't have to support me in my old age, if that's what you're worried about," she said, looking a little offended.

"This is your old age, Mom, and no, I'm not worried about that. I need to borrow some money, and not twenty dollars. Ten or twenty thousand."

She looked at me as if I'd asked her to shave her head and do an interpretive dance.

"*What?* I don't have that kind of money for you! What do I look like? A bank? Where would I get that kind of money? You should go earn that money. Go downstairs and write another book. I'll bring you a sandwich."

"What about all the money you got when you sold Faber Appliances?"

"Oh, that money? Let's see . . ." she said and looked up and to the side, her lips pursed. "Well, first I bought the condo, and then there was that trip with the girls on the Nordic boat—did I tell you about the food? It was so delicious! It's a wonder I don't weigh a thousand pounds. The breakfast buffet in the morning? You've never seen—"

"I know, Mom, I remember. You sent me pictures of all the food. But you must have gotten a lot more than that."

"I did, but it's all invested, so I don't have to worry about my future."

"And you can't sell some of the stocks or something? Even just ten thousand dollars?"

"Oh, no, Roger. That's a lot of money. I can't do that. Jimmy Buffett says a real investor always invests for the long term, and he's very successful, so that's what I'm doing. I can't just go and sell it."

"Are you sure? Because things are really getting difficult right now."

"Don't you worry, Roger. You won't go hungry as long as I'm around. No matter how bad things get, you can always just stay here with me."

LATER THAT day, toe iced, foot propped, a little fuzzy from codeine, I called Lisa and asked her to arrange a meeting with Melanie.

CHAPTER NINE

"Mom? Can you give me a ride somewhere?"

"What do you need? I'm going shopping later."

"I don't need anything. I have to go see someone."

"Who are you going to see?"

"Mom, can you just give me a ride?"

"What's the big mystery that you can't tell your mother who you're going to see?"

"It's not a mystery, Mom. It's just not important who I'm going to see."

"It's a girlfriend, isn't it? Do you have a little girlfriend you don't want to tell your mother about?"

"Yes, Mom, that's it. I have a little girlfriend, and it's a big secret."

"Well, good for you. You should have a new girlfriend. Your wife made a real mistake, picking that Brad Elliot and his big thing over my Roger."

WITH MY mother's Magoo-like driving, it took about three times as long as it should have to get to Lisa's house, but if pedestrians can't be choosers, ex-pedestrians have even less choice.

I'd looked up broken toes online, and the standard treat-ment was to tape them. Rather than spend the money on a local walk-in clinic—the name itself a cruel taunt, from where I wobblily stood—I'd taped my broken toe, the long toe on my left foot, to the big toe next to it. My mother still had the cane that Morris had used toward the end, and she dug out a large, loose bedroom slipper of his that I could slip on without too much pain.

I was surprised they didn't hear me hobbling up the porch steps. I could see them through the living room window, sitting on the couch together talking, Melanie smoking, flicking her ash in a big glass ashtray, the two of them animated, gesturing, even laughing. Lisa let me in when I knocked, and stood aside as I limped over to the easy chair and sat down.

"What happened to you?" Melanie asked.

"It's nothing. I walked into something and hurt my toe."

I couldn't help noticing she was again wearing a scoop-neck dress, displaying her bluebird tattoos and the cleav-age they were perfectly placed to draw attention to. Melanie saw where I was looking, thrust out her chest. "Like them? I have lots."

Lisa sat down, focused entirely on the business at hand. "So," she said. "You'll do it?"

"I'll talk about it. I'm not promising anything."

"Oh, you have to!" Melanie said. "Why won't you help me?"

"I just need to know that . . ." I didn't know what I needed to know, but I was hoping to hear something from them, anything, that would help me think this was okay.

"Roger, it's the right thing to do," Lisa said. "If you could have heard Melanie when she first told me about it, you wouldn't hesitate, I swear. Melanie, just tell Roger what you told me."

"About her stroke? Yeah, okay." Melanie turned to look me in the eyes. "The thing is, Roger, you don't understand how terrible this is. Ever since she had her stroke last year, she's been like—I don't even know what she's like! It's just awful. Her body doesn't work anymore, her whole one side is, like, dead already, and the other side is kind of fucked up too."

"Don't people recover from strokes?" I asked. "Isn't there physical therapy? Or something?"

"Not with this kind of stroke. This is the really bad kind of stroke. It almost killed her, and now it's like that movie? About the butterfly guy? It's exactly like that. It's like she's trapped in there, and I know she wants somebody to help her get out."

"*The Diving Bell and the Butterfly*. It was actually a book first, French, but . . ." I trailed off, silenced by the sound of my own irrelevance.

"Yes, Roger, like that," Lisa said.

"She's barely conscious," Melanie said, "and suffering constantly. She's like a vegetable, almost. I know she'd kill herself, if she could."

"See, Roger?" Lisa said. "Melanie needs you to do this for her. And her mother needs you to do this. You'd be doing a good thing, for both of them."

"And for my daughter!" Melanie said. "I'd be able to send her to a better school, and we could move into a nicer house. Lisa showed me this cute little—"

"Okay, Melanie," Lisa said, cutting her off. "So, what do you think, Roger?"

"And the money?" I asked.

Lisa looked a bit disappointed that I brought it up, Melanie less so.

"You'll get the money. Half my commission. Eight thousand, if it goes for what I think it will," Lisa said.

I didn't think about it any further. I chose not to think about it at all. "Okay. I'll do it."

"Thank you!" Melanie said, a big smile on her face. "I'm so glad!"

"We've worked it all out, Roger," Lisa said. "It's going to be a little complicated, but we've figured it out."

Melanie's mother, they explained, had home healthcare aides. Lucita, the one who worked the weekend day shift, liked talking to Melanie, and Melanie was going to take her into the kitchen and keep her busy while I took care of her mother. We agreed to do it the next day, Sunday, while Lisa watched Melanie's daughter. We'd arrive after Lucita had given her mother her morning medication, when the aide usually took a break.

There wasn't much to say after that, and I asked Lisa if she could give me a ride home. When she said she had a showing to get to, I understood that ours was now entirely a business relationship, and maybe it always had been.

"I can take you home," Melanie said. "I have to go pick up Abby. I can drop you off on the way."

Melanie's little yellow Ford Fiesta was parked out front. She walked patiently beside me as I hobbled toward it. I squeezed myself in, banging my toe in the process, but managed a manly barked "Fuck!" instead of yipping in pain or actually crying.

Melanie chattered the entire time she was driving, about Abby, about how hard it was being a single mother, about what a relief it was going to be when this was all over. I listened from the passenger's seat, my eyes darting often to her bluebirds, and to a tattoo along her thigh, some AC/DC looking script that peeked out as her skirt rode up. Despite the circumstances, I couldn't help being aware she was a very attractive woman.

I directed her to pull over when we reached my mother's house. Before I got out, I turned to her, gave her my best smile. "I was wondering, once this is all over, if you wouldn't like to get together for a drink."

She smiled back, reached toward me. I started to feel positive for the first time in days.

"Aw. That's so sweet of you, Roger," she said, and patted me on the knee. "But Lisa said I'd only have to sleep with you if you wouldn't do it for the money."

AT ELEVEN o'clock the next day, I went upstairs to tell my mother I'd be going out for a while. I found her preparing to leave as well. She had her coat out, and her big bag, and on the kitchen table, her copy of *Eat, Pray, Love* sat next to a white box of cookies from an Italian bakery, tied with string.

"Do you need a ride somewhere? I'm picking up the girls for our book club. You can come along and meet them."

"No, thanks. You enjoy your book club." I kissed her on the cheek and clumsily made my way out the front door. Melanie was already waiting for me. She seemed flustered and ill at ease when I got in to the car. She kept her window open and smoked throughout the ride. At first I wondered if she was going to change her mind now that this was actually happening, but I soon realized that what I took for disquiet was actually nervous energy: she was giddy. She stopped in a neighborhood not all that far from my mother's. I'd walked down this block hundreds of times growing up, going to and from school.

She parked a couple of houses away, and after we checked as best we could that nobody was around to see us, she led me into the backyard of the house next door to her mother's, and from there into her mother's backyard. I waited, out of sight, while she went around to the front of the house. Ten minutes later, she unfastened the latch on the sliding glass door to the patio and let me in.

"Shh," she said, a finger to her lips, and pointed the way down a hall to the room where her mother waited for me to deliver her from her end-of-life sufferings. Melanie left to rejoin Lucita, the healthcare worker in the kitchen, where she would keep her occupied exchanging stories about their wonderful children and their disappointing dates.

I walked slowly through the half light of the hallway, past a group of family pictures hung on the wall—Melanie's parents, bride and groom; a posed family portrait, when Melanie was a child, that looked like it was shot at Sears; Melanie in a purple high-school graduation gown; Melanie, now a mother herself, with Abby—and found the door ajar.

Mrs. Mahoney, another small, frail, old lady, lay in the bed under a knit blanket, asleep, her mouth open. The only things on the bedside table were a cup of water, some crumpled tissues, and the remote for the TV. The room was bright with the midday light, washing out the screen of the TV opposite the bed, tuned to a telenovela on a Spanish station. Dark, heavily made-up women and dashing Mediterranean men made impassioned speeches at each other, gesturing emphatically. Melanie's mother was so far gone that Lucita didn't even bother to leave the TV on an English-language channel.

In a chair against the wall by the door I'd entered was a pillow Melanie had placed there for me, so her mother's pillows would not be disturbed when they found her. I picked it up with one hand, walked to the bed, laid my cane down quietly on the floor. I looked at the sparse, wispy gray hair on Mrs. Mahoney's head, her sagging, wrinkled skin, the pink housecoat drawn up around her neck, and lowered the pillow over her face.

Her body bucked immediately, arcing up, fighting me, but she wasn't strong, and I held the pillow down. Thirty seconds passed, then a minute, and in her bucking, her two hands grabbing feebly for my wrists, she threw off the blanket, and there on the bed beside her, no longer hidden by the covers, were two orange pharmacy vials; the *Times*, open to the crossword puzzle, half finished; a pen; a magnifying glass; the yellow and black cover of *Spanish for Dummies*; and open, facedown on the bed, a copy of *Eat, Pray, Love*.

I yanked the pillow away, horrified. Her hands waved above her as she gasped for air, not even a little paralyzed.

"Oh my god, I'm so sorry!" I said.

She stared at me, her eyes wide with terror as she tried to breathe, tried to fill her lungs with air again. And when she did, as she drew in a deep breath, opened her mouth wide to scream, to call for help, I understood in a flash that everything had changed.

I had killed Mrs. Capitano, yes, but Lisa would say nothing, because I had been invited into her home, had no reason to kill her mother, and she was the one who stood to gain. But, now, if this woman called for help, Lisa and Melanie could turn on me, deny any knowledge, any complicity; *would* turn on me, had no reason not to; would *have* to turn on me, and I would be exposed as a serial killer of helpless old women.

Before she could scream, before I could debate it, I slammed the pillow back down over her face, and held it there firmly until she was dead.

I LEFT her there and made my way out of the house, looked around carefully before stepping out of the backyard. I crossed the street slowly, leaning heavily on my cane, and let myself into the car to wait for Melanie. As I sat there, across the street and two houses down from Mrs. Mahoney's house, a car pulled up and parked in front of it, a Cadillac. I sank down in the seat, but not so far that I couldn't see my mother emerge from the driver's seat, carrying her box of

Italian cookies for her book club meeting, and the other old ladies, the girls, stepping out of the other doors.

Melanie came out as they went in, stopped for a moment to say hello, and then walked hurriedly across the street and toward me. She got in the car, apprehension on her face. I turned away from her, shaking my head.

"What?" she said. "Did you do it? Oh my god, did something go wrong?"

"What kind of person are you?" I asked.

She grabbed the wheel, shut her eyes, slumped down in her seat. "You didn't do it," she said, more to herself than me.

"I did it," I said.

She sighed deeply, smiled a little, eyes still closed, as her whole body relaxed.

"Could you get us out of here, please?"

She drew herself up in the seat, started the car, but before she put it in gear, she turned to me and said, "Thank you. Thank you *so* much."

I looked away, out my window. How do you respond to gratitude for something like that?

She pulled away from the curb, and I ducked down again as we drove past the house. When we were a block or so away, she reached into her bag, wedged between our seats, and pulled out her cigarettes and a lighter. After she put them back, I helped myself to one, lowered the window, let the cold air rush into the car.

"Did she even have a stroke?" I asked.

"Yes! Of course! But . . . okay, it wasn't that bad? But the doctor said she would have another one. A worse one."

"Could have or would have?"

"She was seventy-six. If it wasn't a stroke, it would have been something else, right?" She looked over at me anxiously for a moment; she wanted badly for me to agree with her. "Right?"

I looked out the window. "Right." I reached into my coat pocket then, pulled out the pill bottle I'd taken from her mother's bed before I left. That morning, I'd taken the last of the codeine I'd gotten from Steve, and there had been a full prescription of Vicodin sitting right there next to her. I'd be needing them more than she was going to. I took out two and dry-swallowed them.

Far away, behind us, I heard the sound of a siren.

An hour or so after Melanie had dropped me off at my mother's house, I was sitting in the kitchen drinking coffee when I heard a car outside. A minute later, the front door opened and my mother came in, accompanied by two of her friends, all of them chattering. It wasn't as if I hadn't anticipated this, and I'd have scurried down to my cave before they arrived, remained lurking there until they were gone, but for the pills I had taken, much stronger than the codeine I'd gotten from Steve. They made me slow to react and were now filling me with a completely inappropriate sense of well-being and uncharacteristic goodwill toward my fellow man. Though I was aware in some distant way that in my current state I might slip up, say the wrong thing, everything felt fine, and their arrival caused me no alarm. It is possible that at that moment, at what I assume was the peak delivery of opioids to my system, I was incapable of alarm.

They, however, were understandably excited and upset.

"Hi, Mom," I said, as I limped out of the kitchen to greet her. Their conversation stopped.

"Roger!" my mother said, as three sets of aged eyes turned on me. "I didn't know you were here."

"Yep, it was just a quick thing. How was your book group?"

"A terrible thing happened, Roger. Mary Mahoney passed away! Right when we got there!"

"She didn't pass away, Ida. She dropped dead," one of the women said, as she took off her coat.

"Shush!" my mother said. "We all know what happened, Sylvia. We don't have to make it sound worse."

"You shush," Sylvia said. "We don't have to make it sound as if doves and angels carried her off to heaven either. She died." Sylvia was a well put together, tallish, thick-waisted woman in a proper-looking tweedy skirt and jacket over a white blouse, her gray hair set in an unmoving pouf. She went to the couch and sat down, her handbag on her lap.

The other woman sat next to her. She was tiny, birdlike, wearing jeans and a cable-knit sweater that looked as if she might have made it herself, white hair in a braid down her back. "Did you see the look on her face? She looked scared. Do you think she saw something before she died? On the other side?"

"Oh, stop it, Fran. She didn't look scared, she looked dead," Sylvia said.

"Well, I think going in your sleep is probably very peaceful, and I don't care what either of you say," my mother told them. "I'm going to make us some coffee."

"That's okay, Mom. I'll make it," I volunteered. Even through the narcotic cushioning, the conversation was making me uneasy, and I seized on the opportunity to politely leave.

"You both know my helpful son, Roger," my mother said proudly, despite her consternation. "He's come to stay with me for a while."

"It's so nice of you to take the time to visit your mother," Fran said, smiling at me. "She's told us all about your busy life."

While she was speaking, Sylvia was looking at me, also smiling, but not in a particularly friendly way. "Are you going to try marriage counseling, or is it past that?" she asked.

I looked over at my mother.

"I didn't say a word, Roger, I swear. With all the craziness, I didn't tell them anything! Your mother does not talk out of school."

Sylvia laughed. "Just a guess."

"Sylvia's very smart, Roger. She worked in a lawyer's office."

"So did the cleaning ladies, Ida," Sylvia said.

"Oh, stop, Sylvia. Come, Roger. Let's make coffee for the girls."

In the kitchen, as I filled the machine with water and measured out coffee, my mother told me about the scene I'd left.

"Lucita was so upset! She went to get Mary for our group and came back crying. I was the one who called the ambulance, on my iPhone. We were all in the bedroom when they got there and—"

I interrupted her, suddenly stricken with a fear strong enough to wash away any sense of well-being. "Not the police? Did the police come too?"

My mother stopped, looked at me, taken aback.

"No. Should I call them now?'

"No. Don't call them now. What did the EMTs say?"

"The who?" she asked, not paying attention. "Maybe I should call the police? I'll ask Sylvia—"

"The ambulance drivers—what did they say?"

"They said it was heart failure."

"Then you don't have to call the police, do you?"

"Yes, you're right. They're professionals, they would know, wouldn't they?"

Could you get fingerprints off of a pillowcase? It hadn't occurred to me before.

"Yes," I said soothingly, "they know what they're doing. They do this every day."

"Of course they do. And they seemed like such nice young people. Very professional."

She seemed satisfied, and I had the coffee maker set up and brewing by then. "Coffee's on," I told her. "I have to go downstairs and make some phone calls for work."

"Thank you for your help, Roger. You're a good boy."

"Thanks, Mom," I said, and headed down to my lair, where I immediately called Melanie to ask her to get the pillow out of the house. She did not answer the phone. Lisa, however, picked up immediately. I shared all my misgivings with her, in great detail, perhaps rambling a bit, and she cut me off mid-misgiving to insist that everything had gone just as we'd hoped, that it would all be fine.

I spent the next hours attempting to work and getting nowhere, my brain muddled and agitated, from the drugs and from my fears, alternately contemplating horrible futures and talking myself down from them. I was plainly too old to go to jail. I would not do well there. I wouldn't get sent to one of those minimum-security prisons with my fellow professionals either. This was not a white-collar crime. No, this was murder, a real gen-pop crime, and while I'd never believed the whole "short-eyes" thing, that violent criminals singled out child molesters for the worst punishment, I wouldn't be surprised if they singled out killers of old ladies. They might not have kids, my fellow violent offenders, but they all had mothers.

If I were caught and convicted, I'd have to consider killing myself.

I wondered how many Vicodin I should hoard against that possibility, and discovered Google's anti-suicide bias. It was like going to one of those church-sponsored abortion-counseling services. Every link I clicked about suicide techniques led to a site set up to dissuade me from suicide.

I tried again to work, but my mind refused to focus, and I began to distractedly poke around on Morris's hard drive. There wasn't much there, mostly spreadsheets and business correspondence, and I was both relieved and disappointed not to find a stash of porn anywhere. I did, though, find a folder with the label "Novel." Inside, a dozen or so Word documents, the component chapters of the novel I had not gotten around to reading. Now, glad for the distraction, I did. It was called *His Sins Were These*. It was about a suburban husband who was remembering successive reincarnations down through history, all of which ultimately resolved to the concerns of a middle-aged suburban husband. It was both tedious and overwrought, and there were few sentences that didn't make a wrong turn somewhere, but there was something car-crash fascinating about the enterprise. I spent an hour or so watching his character contemplate himself over and over, and even though nothing ever really happened, it was thick with the throbbing, overheated, Sirkian melodrama of the title.

When I tried to get back to work, death and money and prison continued to distract me. Before too long it occurred to me that what I needed, the thing that would help me focus, was a cigarette. While I'd long ago accepted that smoking is for the young, for when you still believed you had an endless wealth of years to gamble with, these were extraordinary times.

I considered asking my mother for the keys to her car, but didn't want to get into a conversation with her about smoking, or her dead friend, or anything else. Instead, I gathered my coat and my cane, and though the throbbing in my toe was muffled behind a velvet curtain of Vicodin, I pocketed the vial against the walk ahead. I made my way up the stairs slowly, by necessity, but also quietly, to make sure my mother's friends had left, and found her alone in the living room, snoring in an armchair, a book open on her lap. I didn't want to wake her, so I helped myself to a twenty from her pocketbook.

It was getting toward late afternoon, the sky already darkening, as I slowly made my tripod way through the neighborhood; as long as I landed on my heel, was careful not to jar my toe, it wasn't so bad. Still, it was properly dusk by the time I made it across Jerusalem Avenue and approached the brightly lit windows of the 7-Eleven.

"Hey, mister," a voice called out to me. In the unlit alley between the 7-Eleven and the gray cinder block of the gas station next door, two kids, teenagers, lurked. I stopped, looked their way, waited for them to approach. One of them looked at me imploringly and asked, "Could you come here, sir?"

Annoyed and slightly foggy, I didn't see a reason to do that.

"Come on, dude. Don't be a dick," said the other one. A girl, I saw now. She lifted her head, indicating the lone red-tunicked employee visible inside the store, behind the counter. "We don't want him to see us."

Reasonable enough, so I hobbled over, followed them around the corner into the alley, where another kid waited, sitting on a skateboard, smoking, one earbud in, the other hanging down, looped over his other ear. He looked up at me, lifted a hand in greeting. The first two were waiflike, Belle and Sebastian types in hooded sweatshirts. This one looked big, solid, in a beat-up army jacket.

"Yes?" I said.

The girl waif put the drawstring from the hood of her sweatshirt in her mouth and stared at me from makeup-darkened eyes; hair dyed purple framed her face beneath her hood. The boy waif, slack blond hair slanting over his forehead, held out a twenty-dollar bill. "Would you buy us beer?"

"How old are you?" I asked, knee-jerk.

"Told you he wouldn't," the girl said.

"I didn't say I wouldn't," I said, feeling immediately and unreasonably defensive.

"So don't be a dick," she said.

I glared at her and she looked back blankly, chewing on her drawstring. I turned back to the boy, waited.

"I'm sixteen," he said. "So's Katrin. But Max is—"

"I'm eighteen," said the kid sitting on the skateboard.

Sixteen was good enough for me, to be honest.

"Fine," I said. "But I'm keeping the change."

The first boy smiled, handed me the bill. "Thank you, sir."

"Roger," I said. "'Sir' makes me feel old."

The girl snorted, looked at me, at my cane, at my enfeebled self. "You don't feel old anyway?"

"I'm Lucas," the boy said, ignoring her.

"So, what do you want? A six-pack of something?"

"Colt 45," Lucas said. "A forty for each of us."

"Two for me," Max said. "We're getting drunk, old school."

"Max is enlisting," Lucas said. "We're celebrating. Or something."

"Yeah. Or something," Katrin said. Max lifted his hand to his forehead and gave her a jaunty salute. She looked away from him, down into the dark alley, shook her head.

I left them there and slowly made my way into the store, to the refrigerated case in back. I awkwardly got the bottles out, and awkwardly made two trips carrying them to the counter. Once I'd set them down, I asked for a pack of Marlboros, and the cashier, a scrawny old guy, thinning gray hair long and brushed stiffly back with some sort of outmoded hair product, asked for ID.

I looked at him for a moment, my forehead furrowed to convey the absurdity of the request.

He pointed to a small sign on the front of the cash register: We Card Under Forty.

"Even so," I said and gestured toward myself, indicating my obvious over-fortyness.

"I don't make the rules, friend," he said. "I gotta make sure you're over forty so I know not to card you."

I hooked my cane on the counter, pulled out my wallet, and handed him my driver's license.

He looked at it, then up at me, and a smile spread on his face.

"I thought it was you! It's me, Phil! Phil Hirsch, from MacArthur!"

MacArthur was in fact the name of the high school I'd attended, a few miles from where we stood, and though his name might have been vaguely familiar, I had no recollection of this old man—was, in fact, having a bit of trouble recalibrating him as a peer; I'd judged him old the way I'd judged the kids young, without conscious reference to myself, and to be honest, I identified more with the kids than with him.

"Phil!" I said, out of politeness. "Good to see you. I didn't recognize you."

"How ya been, Roger? I haven't seen you since we graduated."

"It has been a long time," I said. "No doubt about that."

"You see any of the old crowd? One of the great things about this place, I hear from everybody . . ." and he rattled off some names, some of them familiar, some not, but none that I'd thought of in decades.

"Steve," I said. "I've been hanging out with Steve Campbell a bit. Larry Petridis."

"Great guys, I see 'em both all the time."

"Glad to hear it, Phil," I said and reached to get money out of my pocket, but he hadn't rung me up yet. I don't see how he could not have picked up the signal that I wasn't down with reminiscing, but if he had, he chose to ignore it, dug in his heels.

"This isn't all I do, you know. I just take some night shifts as a favor to my neighbor, Ajay. He can't trust the kids he has in here during the day. They'd have their friends in here, sell them beer, smokes. Let them hang out and read the magazines, make a mess of everything. So, you know, I'm just in here a few nights a week. I got my own business, one of the biggest lawn maintenance companies on this part of the South Shore."

I nodded, threw him an impressed "Huh" at the end, and still I waited for him to ring up the four forties and my pack of cigarettes.

"So, what you been doin'?"

Despite knowing better, I was a little annoyed that he didn't know; hadn't, as soon as he saw my name on my ID, thought to himself, "Ah, the Writer, the one who made it off the Island, who, propelled by his talent and intelligence, made a place for himself in New York, among the glamorous and enchanted"—but, of course, why would he have heard anything about me at all? I was fairly certain I was the only person on Earth who had set up a Google Alert for my name. I opened my mouth, my first impulse being to rectify this, unfurl my tapestry of achievement, the one that would make clear to him our relative positions; a simple "I'm a writer," to begin with. But then I considered those relative positions, him stuck behind the counter of a 7-Eleven, mowing lawns in the summer like a kid.

"Not much, Phil. Things are a bit bumpy," I said. "Kind of looking for work right now, to tell you the truth."

"Oh, yeah? What do you do? I can maybe talk to Ajay about—"

"Oh, thanks, thanks very much, but that's okay. I'm just visiting. I work in publishing. I'm sure something will come along soon."

"Publishing, huh? Like books, you mean?"

"Yeah, books. Like that."

He considered this for a moment, shook his head. "Bad bet, publishing. I see articles in the papers. Nobody reads books anymore." He glanced at the forties on the counter and then gave me a sort of pitying look. "Well, I'm sure something will turn up for you."

He rang up the sale. With the cigarettes, I only had to add a few dollars to the twenty I got from the kids.

When I returned, the kids took their beers, and after Lucas thanked me, they turned and headed deeper into the alley, Max kicking his skateboard ahead of him as they walked. They turned the corner at the back of the store and disappeared.

I set my cane against the wall and leaned back against it. I was worn out and wanted to rest for a moment before starting back. Except for a sense of displacement in my head, a slightly off-kilter feeling, the Vicodin had worn off, and my toe was aching again. After opening the pack of cigarettes and lighting one, I got the vial of pills out of my pocket. With the cigarette in one hand, I opened it clumsily, fumbled it, and dropped the entire thing on the ground. Laboriously, protective of my toe, using the cane for support, I got down on my knees to gather the pills, but there wasn't much light there in the alley, and my eyes aren't what they used to be, particularly at night, and I was still trying to find them all when I saw Lucas's Converse-clad feet next to me.

"You want some help?" he asked, and then he was nimbly down on his knees with me, picking up the pills I hadn't spotted.

When we'd gotten all we could find, Lucas sprang back up to his feet, and I creakily followed; the pain in my toe had become quite bad from the jostling of getting up and down. When I put my weight on the foot, I almost fell over again, and Lucas grabbed me to steady me as I got the cane positioned.

"Hey, why don't you come sit down with us for a while?" he asked.

I was in no hurry to start the walk home, so I assented, but I shook off the hand he'd kept on my arm as we headed deeper into the alley. When we got to the back of the store, the other two were sitting on a couple of plastic milk crates they'd pulled from a stack. An old pickup, the lone vehicle in the parking lot back there, shielded them from view of the back door, at the other end of the building.

"Hey, man," Max said, and lifted his forty-ounce beer to me before taking a big swallow.

Lucas got another milk crate down from the stack against the wall for me, moved his over, and I sat, the four of us arranged as if around a campfire.

"You must be really lonely or something," Katrin said.

"C'mon," Lucas said. "Lay off him."

"Yes, that would be nice," I said, and took the pills back out, took out two, and slipped the vial back into my pocket. I didn't miss Lucas's significant glance at Katrin.

"Whatcha got?" she asked.

"Doesn't matter," I said, and was about to pop them in my mouth when she held out her bottle.

"Here."

"Thanks." I reached over and took it from her, then swallowed the pills with a mouthful of truly vile beer. I handed the bottle back, and Katrin wiped off the mouth with the bottom of her sweatshirt before raising it to her lips again.

"Vikes, right?" Lucas asked.

"Correct."

"Got any extra for us?"

"'Fraid not," I said, realizing that this was why he'd invited me to join them. I got out my cigarettes to light another and offered the pack around in what I thought was a generous and conciliatory gesture. Lucas and Katrin passed, but Max reached out for the pack, stuck one in his mouth and slid another behind his ear.

"We can trade some weed," Lucas said.

"No thanks."

"My brother's going off to protect you, you know," Katrin said. "You should be grateful. He'll probably get killed."

"I'd rather he didn't," I said.

"But he is."

"I'm not gonna get killed," Max said. "Probably."

"Then you'll kill somebody else, and that's almost as bad," Katrin said.

"It is not. It's not as bad, not if I'm protecting myself."

"But you wouldn't have to protect yourself if you didn't go, so you're still responsible," she said.

"Somebody has to go."

"Right, because we have to have a war."

As they argued back and forth, I sat there smoking, listening. It was true: killing was different if your own life was at stake. Everybody knew that, and the law reflected it. If Max found himself in a shootout in Afghanistan, killing somebody else could be his only real option. He hadn't asked for that particular situation, just as I hadn't sought out the situation I had found myself in that day. Somebody else was responsible for that, somebody I'd trusted, just as Max was trusting the military to know what they were doing.

I'd found myself in a position where my life was at stake, and responded reasonably. It wasn't the only choice I could have made, but it was a legitimate choice. The only real wrongdoing on my part was trusting somebody, believing the things they'd told me. I could have not done what I did, but I would have been throwing my life away, and that's not a reasonable thing to expect me to do, any more than it would be reasonable to expect Max to put down his weapon when confronted with—

"Hey, you want some?" Max held out his bottle, and after a second's hesitation, I took it, drank a bit. It wasn't so bad when you were expecting it. A few minutes later, he passed me a joint that Lucas had lit. I thought it might help the pain in my toe, so I took a hit, and passed it on around the circle.

I began to feel I'd been a bit churlish about not sharing my pills, or maybe the ones I'd taken were kicking in, but either way, I felt a surge of warmth and generosity toward these kids, doing the best they could with whatever the world threw at them, and took the vial out and gave one to each of them.

"So, what's the deal," I asked Max. "Why are you signing up?"

"Y'know. Learn a skill. Travel. Money. What else am I going to do?"

"A job? College?"

"No decent jobs around here, not without college, and I'm not college material. Ask anyone."

"It's true. He's not book smart," Katrin said. "But he's pretty smart."

"Were you in Vietnam or something?" Max asked, looking at my cane.

"No. That was before my time. The cane—"

"It's just because you're old, right?" Katrin said. "Do they just show up in the mail when you get old?"

The others laughed. I did too.

"No, I'm not that old yet. I broke my toe."

"Is it gross? Is the bone sticking out? Can we see?" Lucas asked.

"Nothing to see, but . . ."

I'd just reached down to slide off my slipper when I heard "What the hell, Roger?" and turned to see an outraged Phil Hirsch standing over us, hands on his hips, slowly shaking his head from side to side. Behind him, past the pickup, light spilled out of the open rear door into the parking lot.

"I told you kids not to hang out here," he said.

"They're with me," I said, thickly, stupidly, as if that made it okay. As if this were a club, and he'd let them in because he knew me.

"And what the hell are you doing here? You're buying beer for these kids? Roger, what's wrong with you, man?" He looked at Katrin, the lone girl there, and got another look on his face. "I should call the cops on you. On all of you." He pulled his phone out of his pocket.

"Don't be ridiculous!" I said, grabbing my cane and getting awkwardly to my feet. "There's nothing going on here, I was just . . ." *I was just drinking and sharing illegal drugs with these*—I looked at them—*children.*

I didn't actually feel I'd done anything wrong. When I was a kid, I drank beers some adult had bought for me, and someday these kids would be adults buying beers for some other sixteen-year-olds. It wasn't right or wrong, it was tradition, the great circle of South Shore life. It was what one did. Morally, as far as I was concerned, I was in the clear, and I didn't really believe the police would care all that much, either, but I didn't want to have anything to do with the police. Buying beer for minors was the least of what I'd done that day.

Phil stood there, phone in hand, a stern look on his face, waiting for me to continue.

"I was just leaving, Phil. We were all just leaving. There's no need to call anyone."

Phil didn't say anything to that, but he put his phone away as the kids stood up, and before I turned to go, I thought I detected just a hint of a smile, a touch of schadenfreudian pleasure, and I wondered, as we all headed down the alley for the front of the store, if perhaps he didn't have some idea of what I'd been up to all those years.

MAX HAD a car, it turned out, a gift from a relative who had recently given up driving, parked just across Jerusalem Avenue, an oldish, grayish, generic-looking four-door compact. Not looking forward to another half hour of hobbling, I accepted Max's offer of a ride, and got in the back seat with Katrin.

Between the pills I'd taken, the pot they'd shared with me, and just enough Colt 45 to contribute something, I was by now suffused with a feeling of benevolence toward all, which settled inevitably on my new, young friends. The unpleasant encounter with Phil was, if not forgotten, then already reduced to an anecdote, an artifact, something with no feelings attached to it.

"So, where you need to go?" Max asked me, pulling directly into traffic without looking, eliciting a screech of tires and a blare of horn. I had, of course, just gotten into a car with a stoned, drunk teenager behind the wheel. I fastened my seat belt.

"If you just make a right, up here—" I said, as Max accelerated and shot past the turn into my development.

"You live in there?" Katrin asked, looking at me briefly before turning away to look out the window on her side. "Fancy."

The aggregation of houses where I'd grown up was just a notch higher on the socioeconomic ladder than those surrounding it, but it was a notch that people were aware of, a notch that meant more of us went to college, and of those that went, fewer went to community college.

"I'll turn around up ahead, okay?" Max said.

"Sure, fine," I said, and leaned back in my seat as he stopped at an intersection.

"Who's Mary Mahoney?" Katrin said, and I jerked forward involuntarily, stopped by the restraint of the seat belt. In the light that spilled into the car from the streetlamp on the corner, Katrin was reading the label on the pill vial which she must have filched from the pocket of my coat, no doubt a tempting target, just inches away from her. I reached out and snatched them back, put them in the pocket on the other side.

"Is that your mother?" she asked. "Did Roger steal pills from his mommy?"

"*Shut the fuck up!*" I said, my fog of benevolence instantly torn away, replaced by a visceral fear of exposure.

"Sorry," she said, in a very small voice, actually looking a little scared, and of course she was just a slip of a thing, half my size at most, a child, and I was a large, angry stranger yelling at her. Max and Lucas had turned, startled, to look at me from the front seat.

I got control of myself, apologized, explained no, it was not my mother, she was a family friend, a sick family friend, and I only yelled because I was so worried about her, not bothering to explain how concern for somebody led to me walking around with her pain pills in my pocket.

Katrin looked down at her hand, idly picking at the peeling vinyl of the seat beside her. "Whatever," she said.

The atmosphere in the car was distinctly muted after that. I directed Max back toward my mother's house, but had him drop me off two blocks away. I waited until the rear lights of the car had disappeared before I made my way home.

By early afternoon the next day, I had managed to get some momentum going, and plowed steadily through the

Minotaur book, stopping only now and then to check local news sites for any mention of suspicious deaths. There were none, and would, despite my anxiety about it, likely be none, because there was nothing particularly suspicious about a woman that age dying in her sleep. Happens to old people all the time. Hopefully, when I am old, it will happen to me. Just then, though, I felt as if stress might bring it about at any moment.

Smoking helped, or so I told myself, but my mother had gotten upset that morning when she'd smelled my cigarette smoke. To lessen the storm of clucked warnings that I would end up smoking through a hole in my throat and talking like "that Tony Hawking in his wheelchair," I had promised her I would smoke infrequently and only outside, a compromise which had appeased her, at least temporarily.

I had gone out to smoke again—in an old pair of running shoes; the swelling had gone down, and I was moving around more comfortably, if still obviously lamed—and was standing just around the side of the house, looking out at the street, when I saw Steve pull up. He got out, saw me, came my way.

"Hey, Roger. I need you to take a ride with me."

My alarm must have been obvious.

"Don't worry, nothing like that. Turns out Larry's car was towed, not stolen. They called him this morning. He says you should come into the city with me to pick it up, so you can drive it back."

I was immediately relieved on multiple counts. Not only was the ride I was about to be taken for not colloquial, I saw my debt to Larry vanishing from the account books. I was still angry at Steve, had not gotten over what he had done to me, but of the various emotions I was repressing at that moment, relief was predominant.

I went inside to get my coat and the keys to the car, and to tell my mother I would be gone for the day. A few minutes later I was seated beside Steve in his aging muscle car, eighties rock on the radio, my cane tucked against the seat next to me, headed toward New York on the L.I.E.

As I watched the landscape roll by—tracts of near-identical houses shoulder to shoulder, their colors faded from decades of car exhaust and disappointment; Costcos and Walmarts and Home Depots as big as airplane hangars, their parking lots empty; narrow strips of trees, the sparse and stunted survivors of the once-dense woods Robert Moses had parted to lead the Jews out of their tenement captivity, along with their Italian and Irish neighbors—I began to feel optimistic, almost exhilarated by the recent turn of events. Once Larry got his car back, my debt would be gone, my options expanded. It would almost be like a fresh start. Maybe I could even get Sarah to listen to reason.

"Listen," Steve said, as he reached out and shut off the radio, interrupting my reveries. "Gotta talk to you about something."

"About what? Breaking my toe? Doesn't really require a lot of discussion."

He gave a resigned sigh. "No. Something else. You know Nicolle, right?"

"Who, your girlfriend? From the Comet?"

"Yeah, her. You know she's Larry's daughter?"

"Had no idea. Mazel tov. I hope you're very happy together."

"Thing is, it'd be really good if you didn't mention it to Larry."

"Why, what's the problem? Not my business, but she's an adult."

"Yeah, well, I'm not exactly the kind of guy Larry wants to see her with."

It wasn't something I'd thought about since I'd been back on Long Island, but as I looked over at him now, at his somewhat dark skin, his somewhat broad nose, I immediately understood what he was talking about.

"You really think that? I mean, he's known you his whole life."

"Yeah, and I've known him. You ever see the stuff he posts on Facebook about Obama?"

I hadn't, but I'd read Larry's novels, and I could see Steve's point. Larry wasn't exactly enlightened on race, or anything else, for that matter.

"Well, fuck him, Steve. What's he going to do?"

"I'd probably lose my job, for one thing. It's not like I have a lot of options. I wouldn't be surprised if he threw Nicolle out on her ass too. Who knows what else he'd do."

I thought about it, about Larry with his virgins and sluts, about the rapacious, dark-skinned bad guys in his novels. I could see how Larry would be a problem for them. I didn't feel like going out of my way to do Steve a favor, but I wouldn't go out of my way to hurt him either.

"Sure, Steve. No problem."

"Thanks, man," he said. He reached out to turn the music back on, then stopped, looked quickly my way. "Look, I really am sorry about what happened. It's just my job, you know?"

"Yeah. But you didn't have to do it, did you? You could have said no."

Steve was silent for a minute. "Yeah, I coulda said that. But, look. It was just a toe. I wouldn't've really hurt you. Not seriously. And Larry, he can be a real dick."

"I noticed."

"I've let people slide before, and Larry tore me a new asshole. Which, you know, I can deal with, but he also docked me a week's pay."

"So, a week's pay for my toe, you're saying. Is that the deal? For a month's pay, do you throw in the fifth toe free?"

Steve shot me a look. "I did you a favor," he said, sounding defensive and a little angry now. "What do you think woulda happened if I said no? You think Larry woulda said, 'Oh, okay, never mind. Let's all have a slice of cheesecake on me!'"

I didn't know the answer. "What? What would have happened?"

"He would have gotten somebody from outside. He coulda just called New York, and then maybe it's not just your toe."

"What do you mean, called New York?"

"You know, his friends. His 'business associates.'"

I'd known Larry's father had been involved with mob types, but I'd just assumed that was in the past, that it had ended sometime before Larry took over. "Are you saying Larry's . . . connected?"

"I'm not saying he's not connected." He checked traffic in the rearview mirror, changed lanes, then continued. "He mention the VC guys backing his diners? Who do you think his VC guys are? You think money guys fly in from Silicon Valley to meet with Larry in Massapequa? It's one of the reasons I really need you not to say anything about Nicolle. I mean, I don't know that he'd go that far, but I wouldn't put it past him."

"Uh . . . how much are you involved with . . . that end of things?"

"I'm not. I just help Larry manage the restaurants. Day-to-day stuff. Keep an eye on Johnny so he doesn't screw up too bad. I mean, I might help unload a truck, but I keep my distance from all that. Nobody tells me anything and I don't ask any questions."

I didn't say anything to that, and he seemed to read that as some sort of judgment.

"It's not ideal, okay? I know. But Nicolle and me, we have plans."

"Good, Steve. Glad to hear it. I'm pulling for you crazy kids. And sorry I gave you a hard time when you apologized. Apology accepted."

He made a sort of undifferentiated grunt that conveyed all at once thanks, understanding, and "whatever," and began to slow down as we got closer to the Midtown Tunnel, where traffic was backed up at the toll booths. As we sat there waiting for the line of cars to move forward, something I'd been thinking about gelled and I came to a decision.

"It's gonna take a while to get the car, right? Like hours?" I asked.

"It's the DMV. What do you think?"

"You mind if I do something else while you're waiting? I'll meet you over there."

"Yeah, sure. I don't care. I brought a book."

I texted Sarah and asked her to meet me, just for fifteen minutes, that it was very important. When she didn't answer after a few minutes, I texted her again, told her where I would be waiting and when.

CHAPTER TEN

I had Steve drop me off at Barricades Café, on Second and Tenth, where I often went to work, or just to sit and read. Barricades was part of a small local chain that offered a more authentic alternative to Starbucks. It had large, communal wooden tables down the center, smaller tables around the periphery. The menu was written in colored chalk on a big blackboard hung behind the counter, augmented with free-spirited antiestablishment drawings and mottos that the staff changed every Wednesday, to keep things fresh.

The rough-hewn anti-corporate atmosphere made it attractive to the neighborhood's trust-fund kids hatching startups, NYU students hoping to someday hatch a startup, and freelancers writing web content for other people's start-ups. Though I was usually twenty years older than anyone else in the place, that was part of what made it comfortable. I went largely unseen, as if I existed in a parallel dimension, occupying the same space but never intersecting. With the clicking of keyboards, the constant quiet chatter, and the lo-fi indie muzak coming over the speakers, it all merged to form an amorphous sonic cocoon that let me ignore my surroundings and focus.

As usual, it was full—it had been years since the neighborhood had enough seats to accommodate the number of people looking to sit in them—except for a small section in the back with a sign on the wall denoting a Laptop Free Zone. I got a coffee, took a seat at a laptop-free table, and waited to see if Sarah would show up and allow me to press my case. When she walked in a few minutes later, she went to the barista and got herself a latte without looking my way. While she stood there, making small talk with the wispy, bearded young man behind the counter, I watched other young men watch her. I couldn't tell if it was just because she was an attractive woman, or because she had become someone that people recognized. She was a famous novelist now, after all, but still, famous novelists weren't actually famous, they were just famous to other novelists, who aspired to being famous novelists, and to readers, who still only aspired to being novelists. The only novelists that were genuinely famous were famous for being rich novelists, not for having written novels.

As she picked up her coffee and walked toward me, the looks that lingered on her became more obviously looks of appreciation by the fact of their lingering: New Yorkers follow a look-away etiquette with the famous. And why wouldn't they stare? Sarah was striking, even beautiful, tall and willowy in her long brocade and crushed velvet winter coat over a white muslin shirt and jeans, her strawberry-blonde hair shining.

"I'm not taking you back, Roger," she said, as she sat down. "I'm not angry at you, though. That part of my life is over. I've moved on."

"That's good," I said. "But aren't you even going to listen to what I have to say?"

"I'm here, aren't I?"

"Yes. And thanks. I appreciate it." I looked down at my coffee, fiddled with the cup. "So, listen, indulge me. What

I'm going to do is act as if you didn't say anything final just now, and let you know what I've been thinking, okay?"

"Sure, Roger. Have at it. I'm listening." She put an elbow over the back of her chair, crossed her legs. "Talk to me."

"Okay, first, the thing with Stephanie, obviously it didn't mean anything."

"To you, maybe. It meant something to me."

"Okay, that's a fair point. But you must know I never meant to hurt you. You have to know that."

"Roger, so far, I could have stayed home and written this dialogue for you myself." She pointed to some random young man typing earnestly away on his laptop. "That kid could have written it for you." She looked at me, waited. "Do you have anything better?"

"Look, I just really didn't think it was that big a deal."

"Apparently."

"No, what I'm saying is that I never thought you'd be jealous—I never thought of you as possessive. You've always been—I mean, *we've* always been, well, not like that."

"What are you talking about, Roger? We're married. You married me. It was your idea. What did you think that meant?"

"I know, but we never explicitly said . . ."

The look on her face stopped me from pursuing that line of reasoning. I started again. "Can you just try to understand my position for a minute? It hasn't been easy for me. Things were going so well for you, and my career was pretty much nonexistent at that point, and I was having feelings about that, okay? I started to be afraid you were going to leave me."

"So you did something to *make* me leave you?"

"No! That's not what I meant. Or maybe that is what I did, I don't know. But it was a mistake. I've never regretted anything so much and I'm willing to do whatever it takes to prove that to you."

"Is that really how you feel?"

"Yes, Sarah. I love you."

She looked at me for a moment, considering, and I felt like I might be getting somewhere.

"So . . . ideally, I would forgive you for sleeping with Stephanie and let you move back in?"

"Well, yes. Of course that's what I want . . . but I understand that it's not that simple."

"No, it isn't. Because even if I forgive you for Stephanie, what about all the other women you slept with?"

I have not previously mentioned that since we'd been married, with Sarah literally off in her own world, working on *Santa Country*, I had engaged in a few brief affairs—a handful, say, or a series, or perhaps "a number" would be the most accurate. I want to emphasize, though, that I have not been withholding that information to cast myself in a better light. I just didn't think it was relevant to the events I've been relating.

"Did you think I didn't know?" Sarah asked. I did not respond, except, I assume, to look guilty. "Stupid question. Of course you thought I didn't know."

Denial would be pointless. When I finally had my wits about me, or some small number of them, I asked her, "Why didn't you say anything?"

"Because I . . ." Now she suddenly looked caught out herself. "I don't know. I was working on the book, and you were being so good about everything else, and all I wanted to do was finish it. I almost said something a hundred times, but whenever I was about to, I knew it would ruin everything. We'd fight, and I wouldn't be able to focus on the book and . . ."

She trailed off, staring at me, and I realized she didn't want to say what came next.

"And what?" I said. "We'd split up, and then I wouldn't be supporting you anymore?"

"Roger, it wasn't like that."

"It wasn't? What was it like, then?"

"I had to finish the book. You *know* that. What was I going to do? Move out and get a job waitressing? How was I going to write then? Where was I going to live? I couldn't even have stayed in New York."

She stared at me, challenging me to argue.

As I absorbed the knowledge that she'd known all along, that she'd kept it to herself, taken advantage of me, that, really, I was the one who had been betrayed, my first impulse was to get mad, leverage righteous anger to my advantage, somehow, but in the end, I just wasn't mad at her, because what she'd said was true. Finishing her book had always been the priority. We both knew that. It was one of the reasons she was the real thing, why I was with her in the first place.

I reached across the table and she stiffened a little, but she let me take her hand. "I forgive you," I said solemnly. She blinked and then she laughed, at how we'd gotten from there to here, and so did I, and as she laughed, her face lost the guarded look she'd been showing me for so long now, and the little lines in the corners of her eyes crinkled, and it made her eyes seem to sparkle, and she'd never seemed more beautiful to me. I felt a tightness growing in my chest. It is possible that I hadn't before understood that it really was over, had not truly felt the loss of her, until that moment.

"You're a good egg, Roger," she said, and squeezed my hand. "But . . ."

"But you're not taking me back."

"No, I'm not. That part of my life is done."

"But you're so much smarter than him, Sarah. How can you take him seriously?"

She looked confused for a moment, then abruptly laughed again. "You mean Brad? This isn't about him. Brad's just for fun. Besides, Roger, being smart isn't everything."

Before I could respond, her phone chimed an incoming text, and she pulled it out of her pocket to check it, glanced a quick apology my way, and double-thumbed a quick response.

I leaned back in my seat, and like somebody who yawns because they have just seen somebody else yawn, I reached into my pocket to check my phone. My hand instead found a pack of Marlboros. I watched as she continued to type, a smile flashing briefly across her face.

"That's him?" I asked her.

"Yeah, he's in LA this week."

I did not want to think about her and Brad. "I'm going outside for a few minutes to have a cigarette," I told her.

"You're smoking?" she asked.

"It's a phase. It'll pass."

"Well, maybe I'll have one too, then," she said, a little playfully.

"Really."

"Yes, really. It's a whole new life. I told you." She looked at her phone, hit Send, and put it away.

So I grabbed my cane from where I'd set it on the floor, and after Sarah made some sympathetic noises about my broken toe, we left the place together. Outside, we both lit cigarettes. Sarah held hers at the tips of her fingers and took small puffs, drawing in with her mouth, not her lungs: she smoked like a nonsmoker. I'd seen her do this before. We'd be at a bar or a party talking to some agent or editor, and when he excused himself to go outside to smoke, Sarah would volunteer that she too would love a cigarette, so we'd all go outside and Sarah would smoke one of his. I'd tease her afterward about what an unconvincing smoker she was.

She saw me looking at her now, knew what I was thinking, and rolled her eyes. She took a deep drag and blew a surprisingly competent smoke ring in my face. "Come on,

Roger," she said, as she dropped the cigarette and ground it out with her foot. "Walk me home." So we ambled slowly down Tenth Street, passing frumpy brownstones until we came to what had once been my home too.

I can't say why she did it, but when we arrived at Sarah's door, she invited me in, and it was not long before she took my hand and led me upstairs to our bedroom. Was it the moment at Barricades when my love for her had been so plain to us both? Did Sarah simply want to say goodbye to me properly? Or was it just because sex between exes, in that brief period before new partners have turned you into different people, is the only truly casual sex, the only sex without consequence or regrets?

I didn't know why she had decided to bring me there, to the bedroom we'd once shared, but as I watched her take off her clothes, sliding her gauzy white shirt off her slim shoulders, stepping lightly and unselfconsciously out of her jeans, I did know that this wouldn't change anything. Sarah wasn't going to take me back. I knew this was an ending, an elegiac echo of the past, a moment of grace we could have together one more time.

A HALF an hour later, I lay next to Sarah in bed, mumbling excuses and apologies.

"It's okay, Roger. It happens," she said. "Probably for the best. I shouldn't have done this anyway." She got up and started getting dressed, leaving me there, too dispirited to move.

She stood in front of the big mirror above her dresser, buttoning her shirt. I was suppressing an impulse to let her know how much sex I'd been having in her absence, when she caught my eye in the mirror.

"Just forget about it. It's no big deal. I know it works, okay?"

I sighed.

She picked up her brush, ran it through her hair, turned to look at me, unmoving still.

"Half the women we know know it works," she said.

That was a little cheering, if a bit of an exaggeration. I dragged myself up into a sitting position. Sarah picked my pants up from the floor, handed them to me as she sat down on the bed. "Look, Roger, I don't really have time to comfort you, even if I felt like it, which I don't, particularly. You're a big manly man, okay? That's all you're getting."

I stood up, gingerly got into my boxers and jeans, hopping around a bit to avoid banging my toe, then sat back down next to her. Despite her brusque manner, she'd pretty obviously moved on from any resentment toward me and had reached a stage of post-breakup affection. It occurred to me then that this would be a good moment to ask her for a loan; it took only another second to realize I'd had this in the back of mind all along, a fallback plan. With Larry's car returned and that slate wiped clean, I could start making some concrete plans to get my life back together if I weren't scrambling for money, and she could certainly afford it.

As I began to phrase the request in my mind, though, I had second thoughts and hesitated. Was I depending on her pity? Is that what she would feel if I asked for her help? I recoiled from that. But that was just ego, wasn't it? Dignity was for those who could afford it.

"Hey, Sarah? You're aware of what Darius did to me, aren't you?" I said.

"Yes. You know I didn't have anything to do with that, right?"

"Of course. It never occurred to me that you did."

"Good, because I would never do that."

"I know," I said, and took her hand. "But it's making it very difficult for me to find work and—"

"I've been thinking about that," she said. "None of this is my fault, but when I read what Darius said, I felt a little responsible, and I thought I should give you some money, a loan until you get everything worked out."

I hadn't even had to ask. Something inside me relaxed as I heard this, as if I'd been holding my breath all along.

"But with everything we've been through, I didn't think you'd want to be in the position of owing me money, and I had a better idea. I know you don't like ghosting, but Brad is doing a memoir, and he's going to have to hire somebody to write it. I told him he should talk to you."

She stopped, waited for my reaction, which was to wonder if I had been wrong about her. Was she *not* over it? Did she want to rub my nose in it? Was she trying to torture me?

She saw the look on my face, guessed what I was thinking, shook her head.

"Roger, I'm just being practical. I know it'll be a little weird, but it'll be worth it. It's a good idea. Think about it. Brad doesn't care about getting on the wrong side of Darius, and nobody else is going to give you any work. If you do the book, by the time you're done, it will all have blown over and you'll probably have your name on another best-seller. You'll be back in business."

She was right, but still.

"I don't know, Sarah. I don't know if I could work with"—I had to pause a second before I could say it, and when I did, it was grudgingly—"your boyfriend."

"It would be a lot of money. He got 500,000."

Many remained, but a qualm or two fell away at the number.

"Really? How much do you think he'd pay me?"

"God, I don't know. He doesn't need it. A hundred and fifty? Why don't you let me set something up with him when he gets back. Okay?" She stood up, leaned over, kissed me quickly on the lips. "Now finish getting dressed and get out of here. I started a new book and I want to get back to it."

WALKING SLOWLY across Fourteenth Street, headed to Union Square to get a train to meet Steve, I considered Sarah's proposition. It was true, what Sarah had said. I really did not like ghostwriting. Editing a book can be a very personal thing, intimate even; you can't just glide across the surface, as you can when you read a book. You have to get down in there, up to your elbows—your shoulders, sometimes—and it can get murky and tangled and exhausting. Still, no matter how extensive an editing job, you maintain a distance, and the writer you're working with respects what you do, or you wouldn't be doing it.

Ghosting is nothing like that. The person you're working for is generally rich, and always thinks very highly of himself, and why shouldn't he, when somebody just paid him that much money for a book he doesn't even have to write? He's generally a self-made force in business, politics, or entertainment, or somebody the media has recently turned the spotlight on, suddenly in narcissistic-photosynthetic overdrive, rushing to convert that glare of attention into the green of wealth and branding before it moves elsewhere. Either way, he is not likely to have much respect for books, because who even reads books? Certainly not anyone he knows. Besides, he is about to have written one himself, so how hard could it be? Nor is he likely to have any respect for writers, because, well, look at you. You're a tool he paid for, and he's using you to scrawl his name across the world, a self-expression hand puppet, and for six months or a year, he's got his hand shoved up deep inside you, making your mouth move as he tells his story.

But I'd ghosted books before and I'd survived it. That wasn't the reason I was so hesitant to take the opportunity

Sarah was offering me. What was bothering me was that while I had been lying there next to Sarah, muttering excuses—I hadn't been sleeping well; too much stress; I'd taken some Vicodin earlier that day—the one thing I couldn't bring myself to tell her was the truth: the real reason I had found myself unmanned was that I couldn't shake the image of Sarah in bed with Brad Elliot and his monstrous penis. I was afraid that until I did, I would not be un-unmanned again.

I HAD not kept Steve waiting long, and when I joined him over at the car pound by the West Side Highway, I was pleased to see that the Volkswagen was in perfect shape. What's more, nobody had stolen anything. While my encounter with Sarah could have gone better, this, at least, was a best-case scenario. Not only was I going to be out of Larry's debt, all of my things were still in the rear seat of his car where I'd left them.

I called Larry from the L.I.E, during one of the many standstills of rush-hour traffic, to tell him I was on my way, but he was out at Jones Beach, contemplating whatever he contemplated, and asked me to bring the car to the Galaxy the next day. I drove to Seaford, parked, and took my things inside.

My mother was upstairs in her bedroom, napping before dinner, so I went downstairs, opened my laptop, and set about editing the last two chapters of the original working file of *A Bewilderment of Echoes*. It was not that long before I sent it off to Rebecca Jensen, along with a final apology for the delay.

Hungry now, I headed upstairs, where I found my mother sitting in the kitchen eating dinner, watching the TV on the counter, tuned to a cooking show where two hosts were discussing the cuisine of India, and the exotic ingredients necessary to re-create it authentically at home.

"Oh, you're here!" my mother said. "Would you get me my other glasses from my purse? I want to write this down. Hurry! Look in the living room."

"Sure, Mom," I said, and found her purse on the couch, down at the end where her crystal swan sat. Opening it, I saw nothing resembling glasses, so I reached into its enormous interior and stirred my hand around, hoping to land on something that felt like an eyeglass case. Instead, at the bottom, I grasped something hard and cold. Disbelieving, I drew out a handgun.

"Did you find them? Hurry, I'm missing it!"

I walked into the kitchen, the gun in one hand, the heavy bag in the other. "Mom? Why is there a gun in your bag?"

"You made me miss it!" she said as the show went to a commercial, promising a recipe for a special savory ice cream when they returned.

"You didn't miss it. That's a DVR. You can rewind it."

"You can't rewind it, it's television! Stop saying nonsense things. And put that away," she said, gesturing toward the gun.

"Mom, why do you have a gun in your purse?"

"Oh! I didn't tell you!" She turned toward me, growing a little excited. "We had a book club meeting today, to decide on our next book to read. It was Sylvia's turn so I picked up Fran and we drove to Harborside Manor, where Sylvia lives now. It's very nice there, Roger. It's not like a retirement home at all. It's assisted living. They assist her! You should see it. Her apartment is so cozy! And there was a girl who brought us tea! And scones! They were very good."

"And that's why you have a gun in your purse?"

"Don't rush me, Roger! I'm trying to tell you. While we were having our tea—they make it very nice there, in a teapot, not with Lipton—we were talking about Mary

Mahoney, and Fran said it seemed funny that Gina Capitano died and then Mary Mahoney died right after her, and we thought about it, and do you know, we couldn't remember when two people we knew had died so close together. And the same way! Even though Mary was doing so well. And then Fran looked me right in the eye and said, 'What if it wasn't a coincidence?' Sylvia shushed her, but the more we talked about it, the more it seemed funny."

I did not think it was funny at all. I was also no longer hungry.

"Mom," I said, "they were old. They died in their sleep, of natural causes."

"How do you know? Is my son a doctor now? Maybe it seems natural to you when old people die, but maybe it's not so natural to us."

"The EMT said so. You told me."

"Nobody makes mistakes? What if he made a mistake?"

"That doesn't explain why there's a gun in your purse. Where did you even get a gun?"

"Well, what if there's a serial killer? Right here in our neighborhood? Like that nasty Ted Bundy, or the other one"—she lifted her hand in the air and snapped her fingers near her ear, trying to recall—"you know, the Boston one? With Tony Curtis. They kill you while you're sleeping! And I got the gun in Florida, because of the alligators and the pythons."

"You live in a condo on the beach, not the Everglades, and you only leave to drive to dinner or go shopping." I'd stayed with her when she first moved in, to help her get settled, and I was fairly certain the closest she came to wildlife was when somebody got overexcited at Bingo Night.

"That's why I keep it in the car! In the glove compartment."

"Mom, you're not going to run into a python on the way to the mall."

"You think you know so much! They're getting very bold! From global warming! And I took it from the car and put it in my purse so I would have it with me, God forbid anything happens. Do you have any other questions, Mr. Smartypants, or do you just want to make me miss the rest of my show?"

I returned the gun to her purse, and her purse to her, and went out the front door to smoke. There was nothing to worry about, I told myself. They had egged each other on, a gaggle of senior citizens gossiping over tea and scones, probably delighted to have something exciting to talk about for a change. I was no threat to them, of course, and they were no threat to me, because even if my mother did know that I had been spending time with Lisa, there was no reason for any of them to connect me to Melanie's mother.

The timer on the floodlights had been turned off now that my mother was home, and I walked out to the middle of the front lawn to stand alone in the dark suburban night. From where I stood, I could see a dozen houses before the street curved out of sight. A few of them had blue TV light glowing from a window; as I watched, at the far end of the block, car headlights turned into a driveway and switched off. It was quiet here, so quiet I could hear the car door thunk shut from a block away, then a distant jangle of keys at the front door a minute later.

I looked up at the sky, looked up at unfamiliar stars. It wasn't the great white array of a dark country night, or the vast milky splash of stars that hung over the desert, but neither was it the handful of dim, irrelevant specks of the washed-out city sky—as likely as not to move and blink and reveal themselves to be a satellite or the lights of a plane. There were just enough stars visible, this far out from the city, to remind you that you were a small thing beneath a vast firmament; it was a domesticated version of the wild, humbling sight we once faced when we looked up. It was an ornamental garden of stars, a polite zoo of stars.

For most of us, certainly for me, one of the things you learn with age is that you are less central to things than you'd originally supposed; that you are not the main character. There is always a bigger story going on that you might be only glancingly involved in, more important characters doing more interesting things, while you function as local color, part of the setting. Eventually you learn that you are not even in the book you'd imagined you were in. When I was a young man, I thought I was going to be the hero in a story about a writer, something like *Bright Lights, Big City,* or a Kerouac novel. As time passed, I came to understand that was not going to be the case, and I accepted my role as a dashing minor character in a glamorous novel about publishing, something like *The Best of Everything.* I considered it a promotion when I was assigned a major role in Sarah's story, if only, as it turned out, for a handful of chapters at the end of part one. Now, though, what I was having trouble adjusting to was finding myself the unsavory, ne'er-do-well houseguest skulking in the shadows while a clutch of tea-drinking, little old ladies puzzled out the murderer in a cozy mystery story.

"Roger? Roger, are you smoking again?"

I turned and saw my mother's silhouette in the doorway, and before I could answer, her hand rose to the switch beside the door and she threw on the floodlights.

CHAPTER ELEVEN

The next day, my mother was kind enough to follow behind me in her Cadillac so that I could get a ride back with her when I drove the little green VW to the Galaxy.

It had been a dark, sunless day, the sky low with thick, gray clouds, the air damp and close with mist, giving everything a constricted, almost claustrophobic feeling, like a reconstruction of real life in an enclosed artificial habitat. I kept an eye on my mother behind me in the mirror as we drove, the rear window blurred with condensation, and had to pull over a couple of times when she got left behind at lights, or hesitated too long to make a left turn and had to wait for another line of cars to go by.

At the Galaxy, we parked in adjacent spaces, and before I went in, I walked around to her window and established that she was content to wait with her book. I entered the diner, nearly empty at four, and found Larry sitting in the same rear booth, a laptop open and set on top of file folders and invoices, a tall, sweating glass of iced tea half-full beside them, leaving dark splotches on the papers it touched.

He looked up at me as I sat across from him, and shook his head with a wry half grin on his face, a sort of "Isn't life crazy?" look, as if we'd both just witnessed some ridiculous event unfold.

"Here you go, Larry," I said, and set the keys on the table. "Sorry I screwed that up."

"Forget it. How's the foot?"

"Getting better, thanks."

"Sorry we had to go through that, but business is business. You know how it is, right?"

I did not, but saw no point in arguing it at this late date.

"So, are we even?" I asked him. "You want something to cover the trouble I caused? A hundred dollars, say? Two hundred?"

"Nah!" he said. "You don't owe me anything."

I was about to thank him, but he continued.

"With all the trouble you were having with your plagiarism scandal—"

"It's not a plagiarism scandal, Larry. It was just my agent. His idea of a joke. We're having some issues."

"Your agent?" A look of disgust crossed his face. "That condescending piece of shit sent me that rejection letter? Yeah, well, fuck him. Anyway, with all that going on, I figured it was maybe over for you, and I was never gonna see my money. I mean, breaking a finger or toe, big deal, but I like you, Roger. We both know I'm not gonna do any real damage to you, not the kind of damage you gotta do to get blood from a stone."

I forced out a laugh. "I'm not washed up yet, Larry. Just a little setback. I'm sure I would have come up with the money eventually."

"That's good, Roger, because what I did was I sold your debt to a guy I know in New York." He picked up a pen and jotted a phone number down on the corner of a manila folder, tore it off, and handed it to me. "You owe the money to Roman Palombo now. You should call him soon. With the vig, it's gonna be around"—he stopped, did some calculations on his laptop—"eleven thousand four on Monday."

I stared at the piece of paper in my hand, tried to process what he had just told me, looked up at him. "But . . . but . . . you got the car back!" I suddenly wished I was back in a cozy mystery novel.

"Yeah, I know! Plus I got twenty-two hundred for the debt on top of that! It all worked out great. Hey, you know what?" He snapped his fingers and waved one of the waitresses over. "Lunch is on me. Anything you want."

I was not feeling hungry, but after a moment's hesitation, I ordered something to go.

My MOTHER had fallen asleep in the car, and I had to knock on the window repeatedly before I startled her awake. My turkey club in a white paper bag between us on the seat, we drove slowly home. Sitting there with her, feeling every jolt and pump of the brake, I was more aware of how unsure and jerky her driving had become, and when she almost involved us in a slow-motion accident turning onto Jerusalem Avenue, I wondered if perhaps she shouldn't be driving at all.

That was, though, the least of my concerns, and when we got back to the house, and I was alone in the basement, I immediately thought of Lisa and the eight thousand dollars I'd been promised. I didn't know where I would get the rest of the money, and I was at that point thinking I would probably work it all out, avoid having to pay it at all, because it was so obviously unfair, but I had to allow that certain things were out of my hands, and if I was going to be dealing with Larry's colleague Roman Palombo, it would be best to have a substantial sum available just in case.

I had been avoiding thinking about that eight thousand dollars because I did not want to think about what I had done to earn it. When I had first agreed to the scheme, it had been one thing, an expedient mercy, but it had been revealed in its unfolding as another. That money had come at the cost of a woman's life, and while I know not everybody will see it this way, there had also been a cost to me. I won't say it had cost me my innocence, in the sense that we usually use the word, because that would be disingenuous, and it would also be a cliché, but it was impossible to deny that before that moment, I had been one thing, and after it, another. Even if I had not been *an* innocent, in some strict legalistic sense I did then cease to *be* innocent.

But it was also impossible to deny that I had not crossed that line willingly, had, in fact, been pushed, compelled to cross it.

There is a theory, which I sometimes find persuasive, that consciousness is a trick. There is ample evidence that most of what we do we do without thinking. We react to a threat before we are conscious of fear; the impulse that makes our muscles twitch begins milliseconds before we are aware of making the decision to move. Consciousness, it has been proposed, is riding along facing backward, inventing the narrative that explains why we decided to do what we did ex post facto, convincing ourselves we decided to do it. It is, in a way, the worst of both worlds. We are conscious, but without free will, prisoners of our robot selves, creatures of instinct and conditioning, keeping up a running commentary to maintain the illusion that we are in charge, our life stories a construct of denial, the big lie. "I meant to do that!" we announce to ourselves as we blunder backward into the future.

Circumstances had brought us together, Mary Mahoney and me; our paths had crossed in a way that could not have been avoided, given everything that had come before, and what happened when we met was no more in my hands than hers. Mine could not have been stayed by me or anyone else. I had no choice.

I called Lisa. I was surprised to find, given her recent demeanor, that she sounded glad to hear from me. She declined to discuss anything on the phone, but warmly asked me to come meet her at her house.

It took a bit of persuading, but my mother agreed to let me borrow her car, if I would pick up a few things for her on the way home. In the end, I had to sweeten the deal by giving her my turkey club sandwich.

The Cadillac, a recent-model sedan in blue, was big and heavy, a striking contrast to the little green Bug I'd been driving, but now that my mother wasn't behind the wheel it offered a smooth and pleasant ride.

Lisa was waiting at the door when I got there, had it open when I was halfway up the walk. "Come in," she said. "I just got home. I opened some wine for us." She was definitely friendlier than the last time I'd seen her, less business-like as she led me into the living room, where an open bottle of red and two glasses were set up on the table by the couch.

She poured, then sat down, held out a glass to me. I sat beside her.

"I was thinking," she said, and smiled at me. "We had some good times together, didn't we? I mean, before all this"—she waved one hand dismissively in no particular direction—"stuff happened."

"I suppose we did," I said, cautiously.

"It was nice, Roger, wasn't it? I thought it was nice."

"I did too, Lisa," I said, relaxing a bit. I was not altogether closed to the idea of revisiting old times, but I had other priorities at the moment. "It was nice, but I really need to get that eight thousand dollars."

She put a hand on my arm, leaned toward me. "Oh, do we have to talk about that now?" she said in a girlish voice.

"Yes, Lisa, we have to talk about that now."

"Well, I don't have the money yet," she said, in a more clipped tone, pulling her hand away and sitting back. "The house won't close for months. I thought you understood that."

"No, I didn't understand that at all. I thought you were pretty clear about giving me eight thousand dollars."

"From my commission, Roger, that's what I said. I won't get my commission until everything's done and out of escrow. We haven't even started showing it yet."

"But—" I cut myself off before "But, you said!" was out of my mouth, a protest at the unfairness of it that made me sound like a child. Instead, I said, "Isn't there some other way? Couldn't you just get it somewhere else and pay me now?"

"Roger," she said, putting her wine down, "I don't have that kind of money. Everything's tight. I'm thinking of putting my own house on the market. Once my mother's estate is settled, I'll have a little more room to maneuver."

"Jesus," I said, nonplussed at this latest turn of events.

"I know!" Lisa said, as if we were in this together, as if my problem weren't her. "Everybody's like this now. I mean, I'm sorry to disappoint you like this, but it's not just me. Nobody's got anything extra. They're always talking in the news about millennials, and how it's so awful for them, but, honestly, at least they know they have no future. We always thought we did, but it was never true. It was just our parents that managed to save any real money."

That was, as far as I knew, true, but when I spoke to Roman, Larry's business associate, I doubted that it would help if I explained that my circumstance was generational. I put the wine down on the table and sank back into the couch.

"This is not good, Lisa."

"It'll just be a few months. You can wait, can't you?"

"You don't understand. I'm in a . . . situation, and I was really counting on getting my hands on that money now."

"Larry?" she asked.

I looked at her, startled. "How did you know that?"

"How do you think? Steven told me. But, Roger, Steven wouldn't really hurt you, and I'm sure you can work something out with Larry."

"It's not Larry. It's worse."

I explained to her about Larry's arrangement with Roman Palombo, and what I understood about who Roman was.

"Oh, that is bad, Roger," she said, "but I think I can help."

"You can get the money?"

"In a way. I wouldn't have brought this up if I wasn't worried about what that man is going to do to you, but I've been asking around, and you know what? There are *a lot* of people our age in this situation! Their parents are still hanging on, and their money's going to doctors and home healthcare and assisted-living facilities, or they're spending all their money on cruises and trips—"

I closed my eyes, shook my head. "Oh, god, no, Lisa. *No.*"

Lisa hurried to finish, talking over me, speaking faster as she continued.

"—spending all that money on cruises and trips *they can't even really enjoy,* not the way we could, and I know there are people who would be really grateful if you'd take care of it for them." She said that last part in a rush, then looked at me expectantly.

"Are you seriously saying this to me?"

"I just want to help you!"

"Lisa, you know what? I'd rather this guy breaks my legs."

"I was afraid you'd feel that way. That's why I didn't say it was an absolutely sure thing. I could have gotten down payments, you know, but I didn't want to tell anyone you'd definitely do it."

"What? You told people? Did you use my name? You didn't tell anybody what I—what *we did*, did you?"

"No, of course not, I just suggested that there might be someone available."

Relieved, I picked up my wine again, took a sip.

"Except . . ."

"*Except?* Except what, Lisa?"

"I might have said something to Steven after my mother died. But I swear you don't have to worry about it. You can trust Steven. He likes you!"

"You might have? Did you tell him or didn't you?"

"Okay, I told him. But only because I was so grateful to you!"

Would Steve turn me in? I'd have to talk to him, remind him that I knew something about him, too, about him and Nicolle.

"Lisa, promise me you won't say anything to anyone else."

"I won't, I swear. Don't worry. Everything's going to be okay."

"No, Lisa. Nothing is okay now, not one single thing is okay, so I don't really see how we get to everything is okay from here. *Nothing is okay.* And you did this to me! You put me in this position. This is your fault!"

"If you're going to be like that, Roger, when I'm offering you some perfectly doable action steps to take, I don't see what more there is to discuss."

She was right. I got up and left.

THERE IS another theory, that self-awareness arose so that we did not all eventually become asses frozen between two equidistant bales of hay, an inelegant fix evolution gave us to address those instances when instinct-driven automata had to choose between the scent of food that called them on and the predator's scent that bade them flee. Free will, then, or the illusion of it, begins with choosing which mindless impulse we will be compelled to follow.

I am not proud to say that now facing two conflicting impulses—the desire not to engage with Larry's colleague, whom I had to assume was a genuinely dangerous individual, and the simultaneous knowledge that the longer I waited the more I would owe and the worse it would get—I froze. I did nothing. I retreated to my mother's basement. I could not even bring myself to sound Steve out about what Lisa had told him. What would I say? "Hey, Steve. Roger here. You know, the guy who had sex with your ex-wife and then suffocated her mother with a pillow? Just wanted to touch base, make sure you weren't planning to turn me in for murder. Okay, buddy?" How would I explain myself? I felt hemmed in, trapped by what I had done. I waited, backed into a corner, unable to act.

And so I did not call Roman; I also did not call Steve. I also did not consider following up on Lisa's entrepreneurial proposal, even hypothetically, and while I don't think I deserve any special credit for that, if this is going to be a fair account, it is worth saying that I was not tempted. What had already happened was out of my hands, but I would not consent to taking another life. I had been maneuvered, I was now certain, into killing Lisa's mother, and unquestionably lied to and tricked into killing Melanie's mother, but consciously plotting a murder, killing someone who was walking around planning a cruise, was something I would not do.

For the next two days, I retreated to the basement. I read, scanned various websites for the possibility of work, and—running out of distractions, with nobody else's novel to edit—finally turned to my own novel, the one I had been half-heartedly batting at for the last few years. At some point recently, I had starting seeing it in a new way; something had jarred me into thinking about it from a new angle, and it had all started to fall into place. I had a sense of how to arrange all the various notes I'd been making, the scenes I'd been imagining, and how my ideas about free will and circumstance, determination and determinism, were the thread that tied it all together. I was able to discern the shape of it, as if from above; I could look ahead and see where it was headed, as if in some sense it actually already existed.

The key was reincarnation. I wanted to capture the human condition on the page and imbue those pages with the things I had learned in my fifty years of observing people flailing against it. How better than to depict an individual trying and failing to get the same thing right again and again? A character born into a series of vastly different circumstances making the same mistakes nonetheless would have the reader on the edge of his seat, thinking, *No, you fool! Can't you see what you're doing? You're about to make another huge mistake!*

What's more, unlike my two previous novels, this felt like something wholly my own. That's not to say the others hadn't been, but when I wrote them, I had been too conscious of how they might be received. On some level, as I wrote them, I was anticipating that; shaping them, almost unconsciously, to avoid giving my imagined critics anything to seize on and object to, and instead give them what I thought they would want. I was hobbling myself by not taking chances.

Now, it seemed to me, I was writing with a freedom I had not previously experienced. Not insignificantly, I was aware enough to notice, that freedom was in stark contrast to, and currently absent from, my life. Working on the novel allowed me to stop thinking about where I was, how reduced my choices were, and explore instead a different sequence of events, things that were happening to somebody else, things now harassing Sarah, it was enough to shake me out of inaction. After going outside for a cigarette, I finally dialed the number that Larry had given me.

"Riviera Social Club."

"This is Roger Olivetti. Is this Roman Palombo?"

"This is Mr. Palombo's assistant. I presume you are calling to arrange to deliver the money that is due him?"

"Well, in a way, yes. I thought if I could talk to him? We could talk about the arrangement."

"Do you or do you not have his money, Mr. Palombo would want to know."

"I don't have it all right now, but if you could put him on the phone, we could talk about a partial—"

"Mr. Palombo likes to make these arrangements in person. You can see Mr. Palombo tomorrow. He will be at the Riviera Social Club, at 107 Sullivan Street."

"Okay, I can do that. What time would—"

"Mr. Palombo will see you at two-ish."

"Two-ish?" I couldn't help asking.

"Do not be late."

LATE THAT night, I was pulled from sleep by a phone call at three thirty A.M. I propelled myself floppily from the bed and managed to trip across the room in the direction of my phone.

"Hello?"

"Roger! Glad you were up. It's Brad. Brad Elliot."

"Brad, um," I mumbled.

"Hey, I'm really excited about talking memoir with you. I mean, really excited! Sarah says you're the best, and Sarah's, like, the best, you know? I wasn't that crazy about even doing a book, but Sarah's been telling me about you, and now I'm thinking, you and me?" There was an unlikely enthusiasm in his tone at the idea of us working together, as

that I had complete control over. It was a great comfort, and I poured myself into it.

Thursday afternoon, I had been writing, lost in the world that had sprung up in my head, and got up to go out for a cigarette. As I reached the basement stairs, I heard the front door open. Footsteps came into the house, at least one set of which was heavy enough that they clearly did not belong to an old lady. It occurred to me for the first time that Larry might have given Roman my mother's address. I crouched there, listening, waiting for my mother to announce that I had a visitor, when the heavy footsteps retreated, and the front door opened and closed again. I sprang quickly up the stairs—my foot was bothering me much less by now—and found my mother just sitting down in the living room with her friend Sylvia.

They broke off whatever they had been saying to watch me as I hurried to the living room window, drew back a curtain, and from behind it peered out to see red taillights pulling away from the house.

I turned back to them and asked, perhaps a little peremptorily, "Who was that?"

"*That* was my grandson," Sylvia said, not a little indignant.

"What was he doing here?"

"He picked me up at Harborside and drove me here," she said, huffier still. "Any other questions, Eliot Ness?"

"Why are you being so rude to Sylvia?" my mother asked me, beside herself.

I relaxed then, got a grip, realized how I'd sounded. "Sorry."

"You certainly should be sorry," my mother said, getting up. "Come help me fix our tea. Fran will be here soon." My mother, inspired by the service at Harborside Manor, had begun using loose tea, which she considered elegant, but she found it upsetting if any bits of loose tea managed to make it into the cup, so she had been relying on my sharper eyes and steadier hands to make sure that didn't happen.

I felt bad about how I had spoken to Sylvia, so after that was taken care of, I made it a point to sit with the two of them for a few minutes, show a polite interest in their lives.

"So," I said to Sylvia, "I hear your new place is very nice."

"It is," she said, regarding me as if I were a neighborhood child who had tracked mud across her carpet.

"That's good," I said, not sure what else there was to talk about. Maybe I should ask her about Medicare, Part D. I knew that came up a lot.

"And next door? How is he?" my mother asked her.

"Next door?" I asked.

"Sylvia's neighbor, Mr. . . . ?" She looked at Sylvia.

"Mr. Pedone. He's an old crab, and he plays his TV loud at night."

"Roger, he watches awful things," my mother said, then switched to her loud, showy whisper. "*Sex things.*"

"And you can't ask him to turn it down?" I asked Sylvia.

"I don't want to talk to him. He has been very rude to me. I call the girl to come and speak to him, but as soon as she's gone, he turns it up again."

"Well, I think you've been very patient and fair," my mother told her, "but it's time to call your friends and tell them to move him away, to another wing." She turned to me, said proudly, "Sylvia has friends in very high places at Harborside. It's how she got in so fast! She just jumped to the head of the line!"

"I can't do that, Ida. They're lawyers. They don't have anything to do with managing the place," Sylvia said.

"Could you move to another apartment?" I asked her.

"Oh, thank you," Sylvia said. "That never occurred to me."

"Sorry," I said. "It was just an idea."

"Harborside is full and nobody else wants to live ne. to him either," she told me.

"It's very popular there, Roger," my mother said.

I was looking forward to hearing more about old people and the scourge of pornography in the finer retirement homes, but the doorbell unfortunately rang just then, and after letting Fran in and saying hello, I excused myself.

Just as I got downstairs, Sarah called.

"Roger," she said, as soon as I answered, "there was a man here looking for you."

"Yes?" I said, knowing what was coming.

"He was . . . I don't know, Roger. He was very polite, but he made me uncomfortable."

"You didn't let him in, did you?"

"No. He didn't want to come in. He asked for you, and when I said you weren't here, he asked me to tell you that Mr. Roman Palombo was expecting to hear from you."

"Okay. Thanks, Sarah. I'll take care of it."

"Have you gotten involved in something I should know about?"

"No. No, it's a misunderstanding. He won't bother you again."

"I'd appreciate that. There's something else, though. I was going to call you anyway. Brad is back from LA. He wants to talk to you about the book. He's about to start shooting a movie, so he's busy, but he wants to see you as soon as he has some time."

The illusion of choice comes and goes, and I could feel it slipping away.

"Yeah, okay. Give him my number."

The fear I had felt just moments before when I thought that one of Roman's goons had hunted me down was an illusion as well, or a response to an illusion. A second-leve' illusion. My circumstances had not changed; I just believ that they had. Combined, though, with the fact that he i that I had complete control over. It was a great comfort, and I poured myself into it.

Thursday afternoon, I had been writing, lost in the world that had sprung up in my head, and got up to go out for a cigarette. As I reached the basement stairs, I heard the front door open. Footsteps came into the house, at least one set of which was heavy enough that they clearly did not belong to an old lady. It occurred to me for the first time that Larry might have given Roman my mother's address. I crouched there, listening, waiting for my mother to announce that I had a visitor, when the heavy footsteps retreated, and the front door opened and closed again. I sprang quickly up the stairs—my foot was bothering me much less by now—and found my mother just sitting down in the living room with her friend Sylvia.

They broke off whatever they had been saying to watch me as I hurried to the living room window, drew back a curtain, and from behind it peered out to see red taillights pulling away from the house.

I turned back to them and asked, perhaps a little peremptorily, "Who was that?"

"*That* was my grandson," Sylvia said, not a little indignant.

"What was he doing here?"

"He picked me up at Harborside and drove me here," she said, huffier still. "Any other questions, Eliot Ness?"

"Why are you being so rude to Sylvia?" my mother asked me, beside herself.

I relaxed then, got a grip, realized how I'd sounded. "Sorry."

"You certainly should be sorry," my mother said, getting up. "Come help me fix our tea. Fran will be here soon." My mother, inspired by the service at Harborside Manor, had begun using loose tea, which she considered elegant, but she found it upsetting if any bits of loose tea managed to make it into the cup, so she had been relying on my sharper eyes and steadier hands to make sure that didn't happen.

I felt bad about how I had spoken to Sylvia, so after that was taken care of, I made it a point to sit with the two of them for a few minutes, show a polite interest in their lives.

"So," I said to Sylvia, "I hear your new place is very nice."

"It is," she said, regarding me as if I were a neighborhood child who had tracked mud across her carpet.

"That's good," I said, not sure what else there was to talk about. Maybe I should ask her about Medicare, Part D. I knew that came up a lot.

"And next door? How is he?" my mother asked her.

"Next door?" I asked.

"Sylvia's neighbor, Mr. . . . ?" She looked at Sylvia.

"Mr. Pedone. He's an old crab, and he plays his TV loud at night."

"Roger, he watches awful things," my mother said, then switched to her loud, showy whisper. *"Sex things."*

"And you can't ask him to turn it down?" I asked Sylvia.

"I don't want to talk to him. He has been very rude to me. I call the girl to come and speak to him, but as soon as she's gone, he turns it up again."

"Well, I think you've been very patient and fair," my mother told her, "but it's time to call your friends and tell them to move him away, to another wing." She turned to me, said proudly, "Sylvia has friends in very high places at Harborside. It's how she got in so fast! She just jumped to the head of the line!"

"I can't do that, Ida. They're lawyers. They don't have anything to do with managing the place," Sylvia said.

"Could you move to another apartment?" I asked her.

"Oh, thank you," Sylvia said. "That never occurred to me."

"Sorry," I said. "It was just an idea."

"Harborside is full and nobody else wants to live next to him either," she told me.

"It's very popular there, Roger," my mother said.

I was looking forward to hearing more about old people and the scourge of pornography in the finer retirement homes, but the doorbell unfortunately rang just then, and after letting Fran in and saying hello, I excused myself.

Just as I got downstairs, Sarah called.

"Roger," she said, as soon as I answered, "there was a man here looking for you."

"Yes?" I said, knowing what was coming.

"He was . . . I don't know, Roger. He was very polite, but he made me uncomfortable."

"You didn't let him in, did you?"

"No. He didn't want to come in. He asked for you, and when I said you weren't here, he asked me to tell you that Mr. Roman Palombo was expecting to hear from you."

"Okay. Thanks, Sarah. I'll take care of it."

"Have you gotten involved in something I should know about?"

"No. No, it's a misunderstanding. He won't bother you again."

"I'd appreciate that. There's something else, though. I was going to call you anyway. Brad is back from LA. He wants to talk to you about the book. He's about to start shooting a movie, so he's busy, but he wants to see you as soon as he has some time."

The illusion of choice comes and goes, and I could feel it slipping away.

"Yeah, okay. Give him my number."

The fear I had felt just moments before when I thought that one of Roman's goons had hunted me down was an illusion as well, or a response to an illusion. A second-level illusion. My circumstances had not changed; I just believed that they had. Combined, though, with the fact that he was

now harassing Sarah, it was enough to shake me out of inaction. After going outside for a cigarette, I finally dialed the
number that Larry had given me.

"Riviera Social Club."

"This is Roger Olivetti. Is this Roman Palombo?"

"This is Mr. Palombo's assistant. I presume you are calling to arrange to deliver the money that is due him?"

"Well, in a way, yes. I thought if I could talk to him? We
could talk about the arrangement."

"Do you or do you not have his money, Mr. Palombo
would want to know."

"I don't have it all right now, but if you could put him
on the phone, we could talk about a partial—"

"Mr. Palombo likes to make these arrangements in
person. You can see Mr. Palombo tomorrow. He will be at
the Riviera Social Club, at 107 Sullivan Street."

"Okay, I can do that. What time would—"

"Mr. Palombo will see you at two-ish."

"Two-ish?" I couldn't help asking.

"Do not be late."

LATE THAT night, I was pulled from sleep by a phone call at
three thirty A.M. I propelled myself floppily from the bed
and managed to trip across the room in the direction of my
phone.

"Hello?"

"Roger! Glad you were up. It's Brad. Brad Elliot."

"Brad, um," I mumbled.

"Hey, I'm really excited about talking memoir with
you. I mean, really excited! Sarah says you're the best, and
Sarah's, like, the best, you know? I wasn't that crazy about
even doing a book, but Sarah's been telling me about you,
and now I'm thinking, you and me?" There was an unlikely
enthusiasm in his tone at the idea of us working together, as

if he were sitting there shaking his head, unable to get over how wonderful it would be.

"Brad," I said, having shed some of the fuzziness, "thanks, I'm glad you're excited, but this isn't the best time for me."

"Oh, sure, I understand, you're probably busy. Listen, why don't you come by my office tomorrow. I've got a break at"—there was a pause, and I heard him talking to somebody else—"yeah, Roger, I've got time at twelve thirty, okay? I'll have Elanie text you the address."

"That's the afternoon, right? Twelve thirty in the afternoon?"

"Yeah, twelve thirty. Great talking. See you then."

The next morning, I remembered my appointment at two-ish with Roman Palombo as I read the text with Brad's address. Fortunately, Brad was in Tribeca, not too far from the Riviera Social Club in Soho. After some coffee and a shower, I walked to the train station and caught the 11:05 to Penn Station.

The only real plan I had for addressing my debt was to point out how unfair it was, given that the car had been returned, but I was pretty certain that would get me no further than telling the banks my credit card debts were unfair because I no longer possessed the goods and services I had purchased. It had occurred to me, though, that I could conceivably make some arrangement with Brad that would put enough money in my pocket on the spot to keep me from any immediate unpleasantness when I went to see Roman Palombo.

Normally, in a ghostwriting deal, our agents would handle the contract and payment structure, and Brad and I would never talk about money at all. It was a useful arrangement, helpful in maintaining the fiction that both writer and author were motivated solely by the desire to produce a great book. With Darius out of the picture, though, I would be handling all of that myself. Today I could request some sort of small retainer; or even a loan against the advance, say. The amount I needed to guarantee my safety was small enough that it might not seem unreasonable, and if I did not in the end go through with the book, I could eventually pay it back, but without ever-increasing debt-service fees and the threat of physical injury I currently had hanging over me.

And, in fact, as I thought about it, calming a bit, due perhaps to the lulling motion of the train as we got closer to New York, it seemed to me that perhaps writing Brad's book might not be as bad an experience as I had initially anticipated. Any fears I had about my future sexual performance were probably unfounded. The problem I had experienced might even have been completely unrelated. I was going just then through an ongoing series of humiliations that underlined my temporary fall in status, reminding me at every turn of just how powerless I was. Further, even if I did my best not to think about them, neither Mrs. Capitano nor Mrs. Mahoney were ever truly far from my mind, and there was no doubt an unconscious undercurrent of guilt, and an even more present fear of discovery.

Was it really any wonder that whichever portion of my brain was in charge of my functional hydraulics might have had an off day when Sarah took me into her bed? Brad and his monstrous penis loomed large that day, larger than life, but I had obviously fastened on them as a symbol of what on some level I saw as my own failures and inadequacies.

Were I to take on Brad's book, I would have enough money to move out of my mother's basement, find a place in the city, or at least Brooklyn. Or, okay, maybe Queens. In any case, I would no longer have to be ashamed of where I lived. But, what's more, and this is key, in my head, Brad had obviously become a symbol, a three-legged hobgoblin of the mind. Taller, richer, better-looking than me, almost fifteen years younger, equipped with a vast resource of penile real-estate, and, of course, sleeping with my wife: that was all I could see. No wonder he had hovered over us as I tried and failed to do with her what I could only assume he had been doing a much better job of! But the fact was that Brad had never bested me. Sarah hadn't rejected me for him; she had rejected me, and then she had taken up with him. The two things were sequential but wholly unrelated.

If I actually got to know Brad through the process of working on his book, he would cease to appear to me solely as this constellation of manly attributes, and would instead be fleshed out into a real person, as flawed as I was. No man is a hero to his valet, and even less so to his ghostwriter, no matter how large his penis. The point of the memoir was to humanize Brad Elliot, enormously penised movie star, to make him somebody relatable and life-sized.

Even just the act of writing down the details of his childhood, his early years as an aspiring actor, his techniques and approaches to his craft, the things that had led to him becoming a movie star, the things that did not involve putting his gargantuan penis into my wife, would make that small and relatively inconsequential aspect of his life fade in importance.

And who knew what it could lead to? Once I had his confidence, once he had seen how good I was at what I did, there was no reason our relationship couldn't move on from there. Surely he worked with screenplays that needed extensive rewrites all the time; that sort of work paid very well, and how hard could it be? Have you ever seen a screenplay? They are short, 120 pages, but what's more, they are 50 percent white space and 45 percent dialogue. No need to describe people: the actors are standing right there. Compared to writing a novel, where nothing exists until you describe it in all its specifics, a screenplay was like some sort of magic, an alternate universe where things were summoned into existence merely by speaking their names. "EXT. WOODS – DAY." Done! Somebody else's job! No need to describe the dense grove of trees, their trunks rough and raised, fissures running through the dark, gray, gnarled bark; the amber rivulet of sap that had oozed out in response to some insult of insect or man and hardened there; the afternoon light, dappled and green coming down through the unmoving foliage overhead; the snap of twigs and the give of the springy mat of half-rotted leaves underfoot, where on closer inspection insects skitter and explore and run up onto your boot if you stand still. None of it. "WOODS." I could do that.

But I was getting ahead of myself.

When I arrived at Penn Station, I got an A train heading downtown and emerged from the subway on the south side of Canal. I walked over to Varick, where Brad had an office in a shiny new building, tall for the neighborhood at twelve stories. Inside, I gave the security guard my name, told him who I was there to see. He tapped his screen and scrolled, then nodded, and motioned with his head to the elevators behind him. "Dog Day Productions," he said. "Eleventh floor."

I walked to the elevators, pressed the button and waited, and in the minute before the door opened, I was joined by a guy who walked right past security to stand beside me. He wore large Ray-Bans and a black leather car coat, a particular style I recognized from thirty years ago, when it had been the East Village equivalent of a biker jacket, urban armor worn to project an aura of menace, but this one was made of soft- and expensive-looking leather. I didn't want to stare at him, but I was able to peripherally observe a short, dense, dark beard, and black hair brushed stylishly back, held in place with some undetectable and probably expensive hair product. He did not acknowledge me, just followed me into the elevator when the doors opened. Maybe I was being paranoid, but he had an unmistakable mobbish vibe, however upscale, and I couldn't help wondering if it was entirely coincidental. Would Roman for some reason have one of his goons tailing me? I considered getting out of the elevator before the doors closed, but he took a position in the corner, hands in his pockets, shoulders hunched, without even looking my way. The threat was solely in my head. It remained there, though, and I stood as far away as possible, glancing over at him a few times, as we swiftly traveled to the eleventh floor, where he followed me out into the reception area of Dog Day Productions.

As I approached the receptionist, he took a seat in one of the stylish but comfortable-looking gray fabric armchairs arranged behind a glass coffee table, where there was a spread of periodicals: *Variety, Hollywood Reporter, Vanity Fair, Architectural Digest,* and crisp-looking copies of the *Wall Street Journal* and the salmon-colored *Financial Times.* Behind the receptionist, floor-to-ceiling windows looked out over the rooftops of the neighborhood; beyond them, glimpses of the dark, wind-rough face of the Hudson River, New Jersey beyond. To the left of the reception desk, a circular staircase, leading up. Hung on the other walls were framed, vintage movie posters, each featuring Al Pacino in one of his better-known roles.

"Hi, may I help you?" the receptionist asked when she'd ended the phone call she was on.

"Roger Olivetti, to see Brad Elliot," I told her.

She smiled and pointed toward the staircase. "He said you should go ahead up. His office is down the hall to your left."

I thanked her and ascended circularly, then walked down a hall with widely spaced doors, coming to a stop before the one that displayed Brad's name. I knocked and waited, then glanced back toward the stairs, and saw the upscale goon hunching his way down the hall. My paranoia ramped up again and I knocked more urgently, carefully not looking his way as he came closer. I probably would have jumped when, as he passed behind me, his hands came suddenly and startlingly down on my shoulders, were he not effectively holding me in place.

"Roger!" he said, giving my shoulders a friendly, manly shake.

It was, of course, Brad, his hair dyed for a role. Of course he could grow a full, thick beard in a couple of weeks.

I turned to him as he whipped off his glasses and revealed his unmistakable blue eyes. "It's me, Brad!" he said, with a big smile. "Ha! Couldn't talk to you, 'cause I was in character!" He reached past me, grabbed the knob, and pushed the door open. "Come on in. We can talk now, because now I'm out of character."

"Hi, Brad," I said, walking in behind him. "What are you in character for? You can't be starting *Santa Country* yet?"

"No, that'll be years. Got a whole slate of projects lined up first. I'm about to do a remake of *Donnie Brasco*. You remember that one? Pacino, Johnny Depp? Great flick."

"Yeah, I liked it, it was good."

"Well, I only hope I can do it justice and make Al proud," he said, as he walked over to the desk, pulled out the Aeron chair behind it, and sat down. I seated myself in one of the two cushioned, Nordic-looking wooden chairs in front of it, which put my eyes about a foot below his. On the desk between us was nothing but a MacBook Air. The office as a whole was similarly stark, with a low gray couch against one wall, a flat-screen TV on a stand opposite. Behind him, against the wall, a cocktail stand with a few bottles of liquor, glasses, and an ice bucket.

He opened a drawer and pulled out a soft, yellow chamois cloth, and as he wiped the shiny black surface of the desk, asked me, "You want a drink?"

"No, thanks, it's a little early for me," I said, and watched him take from inside his coat a large glass vial, open it, and tap out onto the desk a substantial mound of white powder. Ah. Thus the oddly enthusiastic phone call at three in the morning.

He took a black credit card from his wallet, divided the powder into a dozen or so lines, and extracted a gold straw from his shirt pocket. He began to lower his head to the desk, then stopped himself, looked up, and held the straw out in invitation.

One of the downsides to being my age is that you no longer find yourself in social settings where people offer you cocaine. I got up, came around the desk, and took the straw from him.

"It's for the role," Brad explained as I bent down and did two lines. "I'm undercover, you know, and if they offer me coke, I can't turn it down, or they'll know I'm under-cover, so I'm getting ready. Kind of thing they'd spring on you, a gritty movie like this, to make it raw. They'd slip in the real thing, let me improvise from there, let me get in touch with the fear of the situation, being all off balance from the coke. I've done a lot of great scenes off surprises like that. So I wanted to see what it feels like, get used to it, be ready to do good work."

I handed back the straw, squeezed my nostrils shut for a second, let go, sniffed. It was harsh going down, but quite good, I could already tell. He lowered his head and did a line, then another.

"You've never done coke before?" I asked as I went back to my chair and sat down, wondering if I might too readily have swallowed all the clichés about libertine Hollywood types.

He sat back up. "Oh, no. I do it all the time, but I've never done it *as this character*, see? It's different. I need to do it in character, see how I'd respond, explore internally how my character would react to the drug, how he's compromised his principles as a federal law-enforcement officer. It's not simple stuff, Roger. I know a lot of people think acting is simple, just pretending, but it's more than that. It's creating a whole life, just like if you were creating a character in a book."

"So you're doing coke in character now?"

"No. Now I'm just doing coke," he said, then leaned down and did some more. When he sat back, he added. "You can tell when I'm in character because I have my sunglasses on. They're a tool, sort of a touchstone for my character. It's a little trick I picked up from Sean Penn, who learned it from Nicholson. You know who Nicholson learned it from?"

"Lee Strasberg?" I guessed.

"I don't know! Wouldn't it be great if it was Strasberg though? Maybe you could look into that and find out? Here, watch," he said, and while I was wondering if I might not get away with an entire chapter of filler on the history of the Actor's Studio, he put his sunglasses back on. Instantly his shoulders dropped a bit, and he sank down fractionally in the seat, his body language subtly changed to say, "I don't give a fuck." His face grew slack, lost expression.

"I do not like to put on a demonstration for just anybody, but I am making an exception here, for reasons having to do with our professional relationship."

It was true. This was not the eagerly friendly man I had been dealing with until that moment; this was a stranger whose hostility was barely contained, somebody who was only just tolerating my presence. His speech had changed too, from the accent-free English of the contemporary educated urbanite to something lumpen, from the boroughs. His cadence recalled decades of movie gangsters.

"Well, come back. I like the other guy better," I said.

"Ha!" he said, and took off the glasses. "You're great, Roger. Sarah was right. Listen, I was going to meet with a couple of other writers my agent talked to about this book, but I've been thinking. We have a lot in common, and I have a good feeling about you. What I really want to do is just work with you and not waste time meeting anyone else."

I didn't know what we had in common other than my wife, but I suppose that made for some sort of bond.

"Thanks, that's very gratifying to hear. Do you want to talk about the process a bit, how this would work? I can accommodate however you want to work, but I've been through this a few times, and I know that there are ways of going about it that are most likely to lead to the best book possible."

"Whatever you think, bro," he said, and got up and poured himself a drink. "Sure you don't want one?"

"No, but I wouldn't mind another line."

"Help yourself," he said, and started pacing, sipping his drink. "The way I see it, Roger, is I've already got a huge fan base, and these people are just dying to get closer to me, you know?"

While he spoke I got up and did two quick lines, then said, "Yeah, yeah, I know! But they don't know the real you, do they?"

"No, Roger, you are exactly fucking right! They have this idea that my life is one thing, like some kind of fantasy, but it's not. It's, like, another thing."

"Right, you're just this guy," I said, feeling we were on the same wavelength now. The book I was going to write for him was already hovering in front of me, taking shape. "Just like them, or me. You've had to work hard to get where you are. You've known setbacks and heartbreak. You know what it feels like to be rejected."

He pulled up short, looked at me askance.

"No, not really, and don't put that in the book. But anyway, that's not the point, Roger. The point is, like, I'm going to make *Donnie Brasco*, and somehow, they're going to think that's me on the screen, even though they know it's not me, that I'm acting a role. But, still, whenever they think of me, that's going to be a part of it. It's like I'm some kind of superhero, like I have superpowers."

"Right," I said, not sure what he meant, or if anyone really thought he had superpowers, but also realizing I maybe did one more line of coke than I should have, that I was a little too tight with a kind of not-unpleasant anxiety, but also not pleasant, and I thought that maybe a drink to take the edge off might be a good idea. I got up and went over to the bar, half filled a rocks glass with Jack Daniel's, drained it off quickly, and immediately found the balance, the exact right spot. He was still pacing, so I poured myself a little more before returning to the desk.

"So, what are you thinking, Brad?" I asked. "You want to break down that image, right? Show them the whole man?" With the calm that had returned to me by way of the bourbon, I realized I was ready for another line, and had two.

"Nah, fuck 'em," he said.

"Fuck 'em?"

"Let's be honest, Roger. You know what America thinks of me. Great-looking guy, movie star, fucks all the hottest women in Hollywood with his giant dick. Men, women, doesn't matter. Nobody looks at me, doesn't think about how big my dick is."

I looked at him, said nothing.

"Come on, Roger, admit it. You're thinking about it right now. Am I right?"

"You just brought it up!" I protested, but he wasn't listening.

"That's all I am to them. They don't care how good an actor I am. Have I ever been nominated? For anything? You know what they're going to do when they open my book? They're gonna go to the index, look up every hot actress the tabloids ever said I slept with, and go read about how and where I fucked her with my big dick. So you know what we're going to do, Roger?"

"No, Brad. What?" I finished my drink.

"We're going to give them what they want. We're gonna give them the dick. It's going to be my dick's book, the story of Brad Elliot's big dick, and they're going to eat it up. Every fuck, every blowjob, every time I screwed two chicks at once, start to finish. It is going to be a catalogue of everywhere my dick's ever been." He grinned, enormously pleased with himself. "The world according to my dick. What do you think? Genius, right?"

The professional part of my mind couldn't help but be impressed. This could be a bestseller. The rest of my mind, as well as my own lesser dick, was not as enthusiastic. I did not want to spend the next year playing Boswell to Brad's johnson.

"That's pretty smart, Brad, but is that really how you want to be seen?"

"Ah, fuck it. Who knows. You wanna do the book or not?"

"Do you mind if I take some time to think about it?"

"Isn't a lot of time on this, Roger. You're not gonna do it, I have to start talking to other people, and, bro, I don't wanna do that."

I realized that this was the perfect moment to suggest he front me some sort of advance if I agreed to do it, which made me think, in turn, of the time.

"Shit," I said, and pulled out my phone. One thirty-five, getting uncomfortably close to two-ish. "Fuck."

"What is it, man?" Brad asked, seeing me staring at my phone, suddenly all attention and concern. "Bad news?"

"I've got another business situation, and I have to be somewhere, and it is not a good situation."

"Oh," he said, a little put out. "Roger, if we're going to work together, I'm going to need you to stay focused on what's important, okay?"

Being put in my place, reminded of who was important in that room, an assertion I could not reasonably deny, ignited a small burst of anger, but I was in no position to express it in the default "Fuck you" or by stomping out the door in a show of dignity. It could blow the book deal and would certainly guarantee that I wouldn't be walking out of there with a check in my pocket. Instead, I went in another direction; I attempted to assert with the tools at hand my own importance, to let him know that I was not solely his pet writer, or at least not yet, to sound my own small, barbaric yawp, which took the form of a bit of macho one-upsmanship.

"Well, Brad," I said. "If you want to know what's important right now, while you're pretending to be a tough guy who goes undercover with the mob, I have to go meet with an *actual* gangster, and if I don't get moving I am going to be late, and unlike a meeting about an actor's memoir, there are actual consequences to being late for your meeting with the mob."

Brad stared at me, a skeptical look on his face. "Bullshit."

"It's not bullshit, Brad. Some of us live lives that bring us into contact with the kind of people *you* only pretend to deal with, genuinely dangerous people. I have a meeting with a loan shark named Roman Palombo, in exactly"—I looked at my phone again; another five minutes had passed—"in exactly twenty-ish minutes."

"No way!" In place of the peevishness of moments before, there was the suggestion of excitement in his voice, a hint of admiration in his look. I could not help but respond to the change in his tone by becoming a little calmer. Also, I suppose, I wanted to draw out this momentary distortion in reality in which I was the star.

"It's true," I said, and stood up. "And actually there's something I was really hoping to talk to you about. You'd really be able to help me out if you—"

"Take me with you!" Brad pleaded suddenly, striding toward me.

"Brad, this isn't a social call, and what I was saying was that I would really appreciate it if we could discuss—"

"You don't understand. You've got to take me with you!" He put his hand on my shoulder. "This would be *so* good for me. If I could spend some time with some real mob guys, I could make my *Donnie Brasco* better than the original! I swear, this is what I need! People would take me seriously! You have to let me come."

"I really don't think that's a good idea, Brad, but what you *could* do—"

"Where's the meeting?" he asked.

"Sullivan Street. Why does it matter? Sullivan and Prince."

"You'll never make it," he said. He pulled out his phone and pressed a speed dial, held it to his ear. "Elanie, I need a car out front, stat. We'll be right down." He grabbed his sunglasses, then walked to the door and looked at me impatiently. "Come on, Roger! We're going to be late." He was right. I followed him out the door.

CHAPTER TWELVE

The Riviera Social Club was between Prince and Spring, behind a metal door painted gray, with a small, square, wire-mesh-glass window at eye height. There were no markings to indicate what it was, other than the address. To one side was a quaint, bright shop of what looked like very expensive children's clothing, to the other a café featuring fair-trade coffees, with two little tables out front.

We got out of the car and it pulled away, and I walked up to the door, with Brad just behind me.

I should offer a little background here.

Sullivan Street is a quiet, unassuming stretch of a few blocks of low residential buildings in westernmost Soho, with cafés, boutiques, and galleries on street level. But before it became a desirable Soho address and tourist destination, it had been a northern-jutting peninsula of Little Italy, and that history still existed there, like a palimpsest. The little cafés that had opened in recent years had all taken Italian names, and while Joe's Dairy—where they'd made fresh smoked mozzarella since before World War I—was gone, in its place was Joe, an artisanal ice cream shop that offered, among its many interesting flavors, fresh smoked-mozzarella ice cream. The empty lot where old men used to play bocce, ribbing each other in Italian, white shirts tucked into gray slacks cinched well above their waists, was now Vesuvio Playground, a fenced-in space where the toddlers of investment bankers played on jigsaw-joined rubber mats, watched over by nannies and a brass sculpture of old Italian men playing bocce. And in the few places that hadn't changed, Pino Prime Meats, and Bella Giorna, a little red-tablecloth Italian restaurant, you saw on the walls stills from *The Godfather I* and *II*, and signed headshots of Tony, Christopher, and Paulie from *The Sopranos*.

The Riviera Social Club was sort of like that.

I knocked, and the door opened immediately onto the dim interior.

"Can I help you?" asked a large, bullet-headed, bull-necked man in a black leather jacket that looked like a much less expensive version of Brad's.

"Hi," I said. "I'm Roger Olivetti. I'm here to see Mr. Palombo."

The guy looked at his watch. I could see its face; it was just now five after two.

"You're late."

"Sorry, I don't want to start off on the wrong foot here, but this is definitely two-ish."

"Mr. Palombo meant the other two-ish. Previous to two."

He then looked over at Brad, who was standing just behind me, hands in his pockets, somehow conveying a hostile stare from behind his sunglasses.

"And who is this?" the guy said.

I looked over at Brad, who said not a word.

"This is my . . ." What was he to me, exactly? Not my friend, nor yet my client or employer, and "the guy who is fucking my wife" seemed precisely the sort of thing the term TMI had been coined for. "My, uh, associate."

The guy looked him up and down, while Brad remained silent, stone-faced. "You bring muscle to a meeting with Mr. Palombo?"

From Brad there issued a small laugh of surprise and delight, and we both looked his way, but his face had already gone blank again.

"No, it's nothing like that. We had a meeting, and he gave me a ride, and I . . ."

I trailed off as the guy looked at us, considering, then shook his head as if disappointed that the world had come to such a woeful state. Finally, he said, "Come with me," and led us into an entirely familiar room, a feeling of déjà vu haunting every detail.

Now, when I tell you that it looked like every Italian social club you've ever seen in a movie, with an older Italian guy sitting at one of the small two-top tables in the rear, sipping espresso from a tiny cup, believe me when I say that, as a writer, I wish I could tell you something else. I wish I could offer you something new, something fresh, something you haven't encountered before. But it was all there—the faded green-and-white-tile floor, the cheesy paintings of Venice on the wall, the religious icons among the bottles of liquor on the shelves behind the old wooden bar—just like you've seen it in the movies, and there is nothing I can do about it.

The thing is, men like this, and every other Italian associated with organized crime in New York, they've all seen the *Godfather* movies too, and *Goodfellas*, and *Casino*, and now *The Sopranos*, and they watch them over and over. It is how they learn to talk, and to move, and what their clubs and bars should look like. It is folk tradition, but it is not passed down from their grandfathers so much as it is passed down by Scorsese and Coppola and David Chase; even their diction comes not from their family and neighbors—

"Oh my god, this is so *authentic*!" Brad whispered excitedly, leaning toward me as we followed behind, his glasses lifted up for a moment. "I love this!" Then he lowered his glasses again and stood back into his sullen slouch, expressionless.

"You," the guy said, pointing to Brad, "will sit over there," and he indicated a table against a wall not far from where Mr. Palombo sat reading his paper, still not having looked up at me. "You," he said, now pointing at me, "Mr. Palombo awaits."

Mr. Palombo now set down his paper and his espresso cup, looked up at me with a smile, and stood. "You're Lawrence Jr.'s friend," he said and held out his hand. "Come, Roger. Sit with me." I crossed the few feet between us, shook his hand, and took the other seat at his table as he sat back down. He looked about sixty-five, and wore an old, brown cardigan sweater over a checked brown shirt open at the collar, along with a tweedy Kangol golf-style cap. He looked at me through glasses with gold-rim aviator frames, an encouraging smile on his face.

"Yeah, I've known Larry forever," I said, aiming for some sort of familiarity, shared experience.

"Me too. I worked with his father. He's a good man. You hear from him? How's he doing?"

"Larry's father? He's fine, as far as I know. Enjoying his retirement in Florida."

"He's a lucky guy. I still gotta put in my time. But the day will come, I'm gonna join him down there . . . How about you? You have any retirement plans?"

"Me? Ha. No. I still have a while before I start thinking about that."

"That's too bad, because Sal here got the sense you don't have my money, and I thought maybe you had something put away for your retirement you forgot you had sitting there, or you didn't want to touch unless it was an emergency, and then I would just have to make you understand that *this* is an emergency, and we could work it all out pretty easy. But I guess you don't, huh?"

"Hold on," I said. "I don't mean any disrespect, and I don't know what Larry told you, but the fact is that I owed Larry some money, but now he has his car back and—"

"Ha. That's funny. He said you'd wriggle."

"Listen, I came in here in good faith, but it's completely unreasonable that the two of you have put me in a situation where I have to pay you more than the car was even worth."

"Well, let me tell you how I see it, as a businessman." I could see where this was going; I almost joined in. "Fuck you. Pay me."

My appeal to his sense of fairness had clearly not worked at all.

He reached into the pocket of his shirt and took out a little notebook, wet his thumb on his tongue, flipped through a few pages. "You now owe me fourteen thousand, four hundred eighty-one dollars."

"Okay, look, it's true that I don't have your money," I said, taking another tack, "but I wanted to come here and tell you myself that I am working on it, and I'm about to come into more than enough to cover my tab, okay? In fact"—I looked over toward Brad, who sat unmoving, taking it all in—"I'm working on a project with—"

"So you don't have anything for me today?"

"No, but I will, soon."

"That's very nice. I am glad that you will have it soon. But we both know that I cannot let you leave here without some kind of reminder." He looked toward the bullet-headed guy. "Sal, would you take Mr. Olivetti out back—"

"No!" I leapt up from my seat, inadvertently banging into the table, sending Roman Palombo's little cup of espresso juddering across the tabletop and into his lap. He too now leapt up, brushing at his dark gray slacks where they were now stained a darker gray across the crotch. "Sal!" he barked, looking across at me angrily.

Twice-summoned Sal now lumbered threateningly in my direction, and I turned toward the door to run, but was stopped by Brad, who had gotten up and was directly in my path, quickly crossing the room. He stepped past me and placed himself squarely in front of the oncoming Sal. Why did he do it? You'd have to ask him. Maybe he actually liked me and didn't want to see me get hurt. Maybe it was something he'd do for anyone in need. Maybe he felt his manhood was challenged, that since they thought he was there to back me up, he would look bad if he let Sal get away with hurting me. Or maybe he didn't do it at all. Maybe he was in character and his character did it. Whatever the reason, Sal the goon simply raised his right arm and backhanded Brad across the face.

Brad's head snapped left, his glasses went flying, and he stumbled backward. Then he straightened up and screamed indignantly, "*Fuck*, that hurt!" as he raised his hand to his jaw.

I could see Sal tense, his fists bunched, as he waited for Brad, my muscle, to come back at him, but then he squinted a bit and peered at Brad. He pulled his head back, tilted it a little and looked at him aslant.

"Hey . . . aren't you Brad Elliot?"

Brad glared at him, continued rubbing his jaw.

"You are! You're Brad Elliot! Mr. Palombo, look who this schmuck brought with him. It's Brad Elliot, the actor! You know, he was in—"

"You don't have to tell me what movies Brad Elliot's been in, Sal. I've probably seen 'em all! Help him sit down. And apologize for smacking him."

Sal walked over to Brad, took him by the arm, holding out the other hand to direct him to my seat. "I'm real sorry, Mr. Elliot, I never woulda done that if I known it was you." Brad shook off his hand and, still rubbing his jaw, walked over and sat down, as Sal followed alongside.

"Can Sal get you an espresso, Mr. Elliot? A limonata?" Roman asked solicitously.

"I'll take a bourbon, if you got it, thanks. Neat," Brad said, his resentment at being assaulted melting under the warmth of their regard.

"I've seen you take worse hits than that though," Sal called out as he went to the bar. "You got the crap beat outa you in, what was that one, *Darkness and Night?*"

Darkness and Night was a neo-noir film from a few years back, shot entirely at night to signal its fidelity to traditional noir, in which Brad had played a Philip Marlowe-like character, trying to do good in the darkness, a lone knight wandering a fallen city, at night, who was also, confusingly, named Night.

"Nah," Roman told Sal, "that was a stuntman, am I right, or, what do you call it, CGI?"

"Actually, I did that scene myself, but it wasn't as rough as it looked," Brad said, humbly, letting us know that it had indeed been pretty rough.

"So, what the hell are *you* doing here?" Roman asked as Sal came to the table and set Brad's bourbon down.

"Well," Brad said, "I'll tell you. Roger and I were discussing a project, and when he told me he was coming to see you, I realized it was a great opportunity to do some research for a role I'm doing. And if you wouldn't mind, I'd like to spend a little time here with you, watching how you two go about your business, maybe ask a few questions, if that's okay?"

"We'd be honored, Mr. Elliot," Roman said.

Deciding to take advantage of the way this sudden bonhomie had focused attention away from me, I turned to make my way to the door. "And where do you think you're going, my friend?" Roman asked. "We still have the matter of your debt to settle."

I turned back and Roman looked up at me. "But seeing as how you're a friend of Mr. Elliot's . . ." He pulled out his little notebook, wet his thumb again, and paged through it.

Brad, apparently bored now that the conversation was no longer focused on him and his fighting prowess, stood up and stepped away from the table, pulled out his phone, pressed a number, and held it up to his ear.

"My original investment was, let's see, twenty-two hundred," Roman continued. "Tell you what. Give me five grand and we'll call the matter closed. A bad investment for me, but we have both learned a little something about life. How does that sound to you, Roger?"

"That's great, thanks, but—don't get me wrong—but I'm still going to need a little time—" I said, but before I could continue, Brad started speaking.

"Elanie, I want you to draw five thousand from petty cash and get it to me right now. That's right, same address. Expense it to Dog Day, under research." He looked over at Roman and added, "And why don't you get me a headshot to sign—no, not those . . . Right, the new ones."

Sal sort of bounced on his heels, half raised his hand, and Brad glanced over his way.

"Make it two headshots. Okay, thanks." He put his phone back in his pocket and looked at Roman. "So, everything copacetic?"

"Fine with me," Roman said.

"Excuse me for a minute," Brad said. He walked over to me, put an arm around my shoulder, steered me toward the door. "Call it a signing bonus," he said. "Does that work for you?"

"Brad, I can't tell you how much I appreciate this, but I'm still not entirely sure I'm going to do the book."

We'd reached the door and he released my shoulder and turned to me. "Tell you what. I'll have my agent draw up a contract and Elanie'll get it over to you. You sign, it's a bonus. You don't sign, it's a loan."

"Brad, this is so generous of you—"

"And if you don't pay me back, maybe I'll have my new friends here come around to collect."

I stared at him. I believe my mouth was open, but I heard no words coming out of it.

"Ha! Just kidding," he said, and punched me in the arm. "I'm sure you'll do the right thing, one way or another."

CHAPTER THIRTEEN

I had not thought I would ever say this, but as I sank into the half-comfortable seat of the 4:01 to Seaford, I was filled with relief at the prospect of getting away from the city and back to Long Island. I was coming from a stressful encounter, of course, and the effects of the coke I'd done earlier were finally out of my system, but that didn't fully explain the sense of relaxation I felt.

I'd left the Riviera Social Club, walked down to Spring and got on the C train, which was held up twice heading uptown, each time leaving me entombed underground, standing shoulder to shoulder in a subway car filled with disinterested strangers. I got out at Twenty-Third, before it could happen again, and walked the last ten blocks up Eighth. I hadn't needed the cane for a few days, but around Thirtieth Street, my toe began to throb and slow me down. With the dirty, gum-stained sidewalks, the weight of the buildings looming above me, the crowds pushing and hurrying past, I was suddenly having trouble seeing the appeal of New York.

Now, as the train began to move—so slowly and smoothly at first that, looking out the window, it was hard to overcome the illusion that it was the platform moving, rolling steadily backward—a space seemed to open up in my chest, a space I was a little surprised to realize was related to the more open landscape and slower pace of where I was headed.

For years now, I'd been insulated from the jostling, posturing, hustle of New York: a rent-stabilized apartment, then the brownstone Sarah bought; a steady, adequate income funneled my way by Darius; a comfortable, unchallenging, midlevel status in my profession. All of that had been torn away from me, and I'd been thrown back into the city's mixed-martial-arts cage match, uprooted, scrambling for work, competing with the antlered masculinity of Brad, Sal, Mr. Palombo. I honestly didn't know that I was still up to it, or even if I were, that I saw the point. Maybe it was time to look for something else. Not the Long Island suburbs, of course, but something more like them than New York—

"Excuse me, is this seat taken?"

I was slumped against the window, taking up a little more room than I was entitled to. The "Excuse me" was a formality more than a question, a request that I yield the extra space I was occupying. I straightened up, slid over, made myself more compact.

She was what Larry would have called "classy." Around my age, pretty, with neatly styled, shoulder-length, ash-blonde hair, the kind of coloring that suggested gray without being gray, a color that said, "We all know I'm gray, but I like this better." Makeup that looked like she wasn't wearing makeup. An Eileen Fisher outfit that allowed she had an excellent figure without calling too much attention to it. She looked exactly like the tastefully younger wife in an ad you'd see in the *New Yorker*, walking hand in hand through the autumnal dunes with her recently retired executive husband, his life companion and reward for having invested so wisely.

Sitting up now, I couldn't help noticing that the train was in no way crowded, and there were many other seats available that she might have chosen. The thing is, it had been a while. Weeks, if you don't count the abortive encounter with Sarah, which I would have liked not to count, would have liked, in fact, to forget entirely. This seemed as if it might be an opportunity dropped in my lap to forget it, to make it not my most recent and prominent memory. I turned to her and smiled.

She smiled back and took out her book, *Wolf Hall*, and opened it about a hundred pages in.

"Great book," I said. "But it would have helped if she didn't refer to every character as 'he.'"

She smiled again. "I know! Sometimes I'll be reading for a whole page before I'm sure who I'm reading about."

"Worth it, though."

"Yes," she said, smiled again, and started reading. I turned to look back out the window, wondering if I had misjudged the situation, but a few minutes later she closed the book in her lap and said, "I'm Anna."

"Roger," I said, and shook her small, elegant hand. There was no wedding ring.

She was a lawyer with an insurance company, I soon learned, and a big reader of the better kind of books. I told her about my work, mentioned some novels I'd worked on, though not *Santa Country*. However, I was not above mentioning the book I was doing with Brad Elliot, even if I had not yet committed to doing it, because reflected glory is still glory, and it highlights whatever shine you have yourself. Besides, everyone likes to hear about movie stars, no matter how classy they are.

By the time we were approaching my station, we had exchanged numbers, and I knew she had grown up in Alabama, gone to NYU Law, and had recently divorced her recently retired husband, a corporate lawyer who had taken up with a much younger paralegal as part of his retirement package. There was a reason the wives in those ads were never more than tastefully younger; the *New Yorker* has many female readers, and nobody responds well to having their face rubbed in the real world.

"Well, he's obviously a tasteless oaf, and will soon regret it," I said as we pulled into the Seaford station. As the doors opened, I took a calculated risk and remained in my seat.

"Oh, hell," I exclaimed a minute later as the train pulled out of the station. I explained that I had been so caught up in the conversation that I had missed my stop. Her stop was Massapequa Park, two farther on, where she had a house in a tonier area, right on the water, a ten-minute drive away. She looked at me, made a final assessment, then took her own calculated risk. Her car was at the station, and she offered me a ride home.

She had to stop at her house first, of course, and as long as we were there we might as well have some of the wine she'd opened the night before. Less than an hour later, we were in bed.

I suppose she'd had practice with her older, retirement-aged husband, because she was much more comforting than Sarah had been. Fortunately, I was prepared for this possibility, had in fact been expecting it, and this time I had a backup plan and was not too thrown to enact it. There are other things you can do in bed, and I've had a lot of practice, so I tried to make sure Anna did not feel shortchanged. She seemed to appreciate it (twice), and she insisted that it was all okay, but I knew better. This was definitely not okay. Since my meeting with Brad, his dick had only grown in my imagination, claimed more territory, and mine had gone into full retreat.

We made light conversation on the ride back to my mother's house, and we even laughed a few times. She asked me to call her, but I was relieved when I got out of the car, and I assumed that she was too.

I WAS deep in my novel the next day, as far removed from my current circumstances as I could manage, when an email arrived from Elanie, Brad's assistant. Attached was the contract to ghostwrite the memoir, passed along from his agent. It wasn't particularly complicated as these things go, three legal-sized pdf pages, and the terms were generous enough. Work-for-hire, no points, neither a *with*, *and*, nor *as told to* on the cover, but there would be a credit in the acknowledgments, on which I would be consulted, meaning I could suggest the phrasing myself, if I didn't take credit too plainly. They were offering two hundred thousand, with fifty on signing and the rest paid out in installments over the course of the job. Travel, transcription, and other reasonable expenses to be reimbursed within sixty days.

It was very decent money for a year's work, but it would be a year with Brad's arm up my ass, writing about the adventures of his mighty dick. It goes almost without saying that I was not looking forward to that, but just as much, I was not looking forward to spending a year doing work that I would know I was doing only because I didn't have a choice. However I spun it to others, I would know that it had been forced on me.

You hear people say that there is dignity in work, but you never hear it from the people doing the kind of work that needs to be justified by noble-sounding aphorisms, because those people know it is not true. Such work is in fact doubly undignified, because the unpleasantness of it never lets you forget that you would be doing something else if you could, forces you to be aware of being forced to do it, disallows the illusion of choice, of independence, of dignity. There is dignity in work only when you can believe you've chosen to do it.

As long as your circumstances are not too unpleasant, the work not too undignified, you can always sell yourself the story that you made choices that led you to where you are. You can ignore the fact that the path you are on was the only path open to you, that forces larger than yourself led you down it. It is only when you attempt to turn off the path you thought you had chosen that you find yourself facing the walls of your chute.

There would be no dignity in writing this book for Brad; if I did it, it would only be because I had no choice.

Would it be so wrong then, would it not be almost heroic, a blow for freedom and dignity, were I to sign the contract, take that first check, and disappear?

Yes, I know how it sounds, but bear with me. Let's consider this from a practical point of view first.

I have heard good things about other places. Magazines and websites regularly present lists of the best places to live in the United States, cities in North Carolina and Nebraska, Minnesota and Iowa. New York City has never once been on any of them. Smaller towns, slower paced, where prices are lower, the air is cleaner, and the competition is not so stiff. Surely in one of those places, someone with my skills and experience could find work, editing something regional and unimportant. With fifty thousand as a cushion, I could find a place to live, rent an apartment that wasn't priced for investment bankers and Russian oligarchs. Further, I think it's safe to assume that anyone who looked like a movie star would have already moved away from there to be one.

And, while I would obviously be in breach of contract, and Brad could certainly take legal action to get his money back, would he? Fifty thousand was not a significant sum to him; he probably made that in a few days on set, and it would probably cost him that much in high-priced lawyers if I put up a fight. And that's assuming he even knew where to find me. I know this is not the nineteenth century, or even the 1970s, and everyone leaves an electronic footprint, but if I were careful, mine might be fairly difficult to follow. My credit cards were approaching the point where they would be worth more as recycled plastic, so it wasn't as if I'd be leaving traces. You have to figure he'd be looking at fees for private detectives, too, and at that point, who wouldn't give up?

Finally, and I know that I'm stretching things a bit to list this under practical considerations, but away from New York and the publishing industry, away from the pressure and the constant reminders of who was on top and who got paid what, I thought I might be able to give this novel I was writing a real chance, let it grow and become something genuine, something that wasn't written for commercial reasons or to impress anybody. Maybe that would be the key to finally writing something I could be proud of, something of value, and if it was, maybe when it was done, then I'd have something worth real money. And if that were the case, and I wanted to return to New York to enjoy my success, I'd have the money to pay Brad back.

But that wasn't even the point. While it might seem at times that I've been rationalizing the things I've done, that I'm letting myself off the hook too easily, I was not comfortable with the turns my life had taken. It was becoming ever clearer to me that I'd made some less than noble choices, and I don't just mean recently. Maybe, if I wrote something that was genuinely good, something original, something I could hold up and proudly say *I wrote this; this is mine*, I could start to feel good about myself again.

Now, I know that I haven't addressed the morality of taking that money from Brad and absconding with it, and it might seem as if I hadn't considered that aspect of it, so to get right to it: Would it be wrong? I don't think that's for me to say. People have done far worse things. Who am I to judge them?

LATER THAT day, after a few solid hours of very satisfactory writing—I had four decent chapters now, and I think I'd done almost three thousand words since morning; I wouldn't have been surprised to discover myself covered with a sheen of sweat from the intensity of sustained concentration—I forcibly extracted myself and went upstairs to the kitchen to refuel. My mother had guests at that moment, though, and called me into the living room to say hello.

She was sitting on the couch with her friend Sylvia. Standing near them was a young man with a crew cut, in loose, torn jeans and a baggy army jacket, sipping cautiously from a freshly opened can of Fresca, looking out of place and uncomfortable amid the fussy and precisely arranged decor.

"Roger, this is Sylvia's handsome grandson, Max," my mother said. He turned, and we recognized each other at the same time. It was the kid from the 7-Eleven, the one who had enlisted. I was about to say something jocular about his new hairstyle when he opened his eyes wide in a pleading look. It took me only a second to realize he did not want his grandmother finding out he solicited strangers at 7-Eleven to buy him beer. It took me only another second to realize I didn't particularly want my mother to know I was the sort of stranger who would do it. I reached out and shook his hand. "Roger," I said.

"Uh, hey," he said, then turned to his grandmother. "When you want me to pick you up?"

She looked at the small gold wristwatch she wore. "Five o'clock would be nice, dear."

"Okay, later."

I followed him to the door to shut it behind him, and then remembered, the moment coming back to me like a blow to the head, his sister with Mary Mahoney's prescription in her hand. *Did Roger steal pills from his mommy?* I suddenly wanted to be very sure his grandmother remained in the dark about our previous encounter. When I stepped outside to have a word with him, though, he had already gotten in the car and was pulling away from the curb, the raccoon-eyed, purple-haired Katrin sitting in the passenger seat beside him, looking my way.

CHAPTER FOURTEEN

Back downstairs, I tried to write, but I kept imagining conversations between Max and Katrin, and Katrin and Sylvia, and Sylvia and the police. I arrayed them like flowcharts, assigned them likelihoods: a 75 percent chance that Max and Katrin would discuss me in the car, but only a 10 percent chance either one of them would say anything to Sylvia, so a 20 percent chance between them. Altogether, that would be, what, then, a 15 percent chance? And etc. Did that make it a good idea to intervene? Should I somehow get in touch with the two of them and offer them money not to say anything? That would only point them at it, though. I could explain that it was about the drugs, which I'm sure they would understand, but they would also be more likely to put it all together themselves if the subject of Mrs. Mahoney ever came up, and now I was trying to figure out how likely that was.

I was fully occupied with this when Steve called. We hadn't spoken since Lisa told me he was aware of my part in the death of her mother, and although I was enough in control of myself to put aside the matter of Max and Katrin and focus on our conversation, I felt like I was trading one potentially ticking bomb for another, juggling both frying pans and fires.

I didn't know what he thought about what he'd heard, but when I greeted him cautiously, he plowed right through it, brushed aside the tentative feelers I was extending. We needed to talk, he said, and he asked me to meet him at one of Larry's diners, the one that had recently opened in Syosset, where he was taking care of some business.

After I'd gone upstairs and listened sympathetically to the latest grousing about Sylvia's awful neighbor, Mr. Pedone, my mother was amenable to letting me use her car. Half an hour later, I pulled up in front of a sign that read *The Nebula of Syosset*. Syosset was a twenty-minute drive north of Seaford, two-thirds of the way across the thorax of Long Island to the North Shore, and therefore 66 percent ritzier. Houses weren't jammed so close together here, and the greenery was darker and denser; it was a safe bet SAT scores were higher too.

Accordingly, the Nebula was a bit more upscale, a bit larger, while still recognizably one of Larry's diners. Instead of being set among a string of stores and restaurants along a commercial strip, it was a lone establishment on a less trafficked road, and set back farther from it. The parking lot was surrounded by trees, the signage less garish, and the menu offered more specials involving fresh fish and pasta, with correspondingly higher prices.

The place was almost empty when I walked in. I didn't see Steve anywhere, and so I told the hostess—a college-aged blonde who looked like she'd have a shot at print modeling—who I was looking for. She directed me toward a booth in the far reaches of the main room, and as I passed between tables, I did not once have to turn sideways to avoid bumping into chairs.

Steve was not waiting for me alone, it turned out. I slid into the booth and found myself facing the star-crossed lovers, Steve Campbell and Nicolle Petridis, sharing a BLT deluxe.

"Hey," Steve said.

"Hi," I said, nodding, wary.

"We haven't actually met," Nicolle said, and wiped her fingers on her red cloth napkin and reached her hand across the table. "I'm Nicolle."

I shook her hand and looked at Steve, who was leaning back, watching us, his left arm over Nicolle's shoulders, eating french fries with his other hand.

"Steven gave me your novel to read," Nicolle said. "I started it. It's very good."

"Thanks. I wrote it a long time ago."

"Are you working on anything now?"

While I knew it was unlikely she had asked out of anything other than politeness, I jumped on the opportunity to change the subject, even if the subject I was avoiding had not yet come up. But also, to be completely honest, I hadn't had anyone to talk to about my novel. There is a thing people say: writing a novel is like being in love. It's cheesy, but it is also to some extent true. You become obsessed, see everything in terms of your novel—events in the news; things brought up in conversation; every other novel—and want to talk about your novel endlessly. So I started telling them about it. A rookie move, but I couldn't resist.

After I had been going on for about a minute, I had the presence of mind to notice Nicolle's eyes widening in interest, almost always a signal unconsciously triggered to counterbalance the lack of interest one is actually feeling. And really, who could blame her? Hearing about somebody else's novel in progress is about as interesting as hearing about somebody else's dream. Unless you yourself have a role in it, you are just waiting for it to be over, trying not to think about the precious seconds of your life ticking away. I also noticed that a waitress was standing beside the table, waiting patiently to take my order, which was more professionalism than I was demonstrating. You don't tell people about your novel, I reminded myself; that is what the novel is for.

"Well, anyway, I'm very happy with the way it's going," I said, and asked for a Diet Coke. When the waitress had left, I asked Steve, "So, what's up?" I was not able to fully keep the apprehension out of my voice.

"Relax, man. Everything's good. I have a proposition for you."

I jumped to the obvious conclusion, but remembered that Steve's mother had died when we were in junior high. "Yes?" I said.

"We want to open our own place!" Nicolle interjected.

"Good for you?" I said, uncertainly, looking from one to the other.

"Thing is," Steve said, "we would need a serious amount of cash to start."

This made more sense, but still not all that much. "Are you asking me to invest in a restaurant, Steve? Because if you are, I am definitely the wrong tree to be barking up."

Steve shook his head, smiled. "No. We're *offering* you money."

"Did you know I have two degrees?" asked Nicolle, irrelevantly. "Did Steven tell you that?"

"No, why? What does that have to do with anything?"

"Listen to her, Roger."

"I did a double major, hotel and restaurant management and business administration, so I could come back and work with my father, just like he did so he could come home and take over for my grandfather." She looked at me expectantly, waited.

"I didn't know that," I said.

"And you know what happened while I was away at school? He started training my brother, Johnny, to run his business. My little brother, who went to Nassau Community College for one semester before dropping out. And you

know what job my father gave me when I graduated? I'm
a hostess. I'm supposed to smile and seat people and take
their money. Because I'm a girl. I schedule the staff, I look
over the books, but I've been working for my father for six
years, and he won't even let me manage one diner, and
Johnny's in charge of three places. And if it weren't for me
and Steven fixing all of Johnny's mistakes, he would have
put them out of business by now."

"I'm sorry to hear that," I said. "That's not right. But I
still don't see—"

"Wait," Steve said. "There's more."

"So, anyway," said Nicolle, "all this time, my father's
been putting money away. He's got over a million now, just
sitting there. I know, because I've seen the books. He says
it's for some big new business he's going to open. And when
I asked him if he could help me open my own place, do you
know what he does? He buys me a new car, like that's supposed to make me happy. He doesn't take me seriously. He's
never *going* to take me seriously. He doesn't think women
should be in business. You know what he said?"

"What?"

"You need balls to be in business, and women just don't
have balls."

"So, what? Do you want me to talk to him? I'm happy
to say something if you want, but I don't think he's going to
listen to me. Either way, you don't have to give me money
for that."

"No, Roger," Steve said, leaning forward, lowering his
voice. "We don't want you to talk to him. We want you to,
uh . . . take care of him." He paused, waited for a reaction,
but I didn't give him one. I pretended not to understand,
tilted my head and furrowed my brow, as if I were trying to
puzzle it out but just couldn't. Steve looked around again,
leaned in closer, lowered his voice more. "Kill him," he
said, then continued, determined, in a rush. "We've got it

all figured. We can't do it, because the cops would look at us first. But nobody would ever suspect you."

I glanced around too, then leaned forward myself, until our heads were almost touching, matched my voice to his. "You know why nobody would ever suspect me? Because I would never do that." I leaned back, resumed a normal speaking voice. "And you shouldn't even be talking about it. I mean, come on, Larry's your friend."

"He's not my friend," Steve said, sitting back. "He's the racist asshole I work for."

"Well, sure, okay, he is, but . . ."

"It's true," Nicolle said. "You should hear him around the house. He knows he can't talk like that in public, but when it's just the family?" She shook her head.

"Okay, fine. He is. But so are a lot of people. You don't just go around . . . doing that."

"It's not about that," Steve said, shaking his head. "I'm used to it. I'm just saying, he's an asshole, and he's not my friend. If something happened to him, I'm not going to feel bad about it."

"He makes Steven do awful things," Nicolle said.

Steve turned to her, looking a little offended. "Not that awful."

"Okay, whatever, he's an asshole," I said. "Granted. You're not telling me anything I don't know. But I'm not doing this, and you're not either. He doesn't deserve that."

"Those old ladies deserved it more than Larry?" Steve asked.

I was silent for a moment, a little shocked to finally be confronted with it, and also that Lisa had kept him caught up; she hadn't mentioned that. I glanced at Nicolle, somehow convincing myself for just an instant that she didn't know, that I still had a hope of stopping this conversation before she found out, but of course he had told her, long before we all sat down together. I shook my head, almost violently. "That was *different*, and you know it! They were old, and sick, and anyway, if I'd known the whole story, I never would have done it."

Nobody said anything.

"You know that, right? Lisa *tricked* me! I didn't mean to—"

"Hey, man, relax. We're not saying you did anything wrong. Lisa's mother, she was just about gone anyway. When Lisa asked me to do it—"

"She asked *you* to do it?"

"Yeah. Remember I told you we had that big fight? When she told me about all the young guys she was meeting online? That's what we were fighting about. I mean, I could see her point, but I wasn't going to do it, no matter what she said. Not my problem. But she wouldn't let up, she kept bringing it up again, and then she just suddenly dropped it. When you told me you were sleeping with her, I figured she'd asked you. Then she told me you did it, and then that other one. She bragged about it, you wanna know the truth."

I would have been reeling if I hadn't imagined this conversation a dozen times already in one form or another. "Okay, but that doesn't mean I'm going to do this. I'm not some"—quick glance around again, and then I lowered my voice—"murderer for hire."

Steve tilted his head a little to the side. "You kind of are."

"No, I am not, and I'm not doing this."

"You kind of have to," he said, conclusively, and let the threat hang there between us.

"No," I said slowly. "No, I don't. You have no proof of anything. You can't go to the police. The only way I get in trouble for this is if Lisa says I did it, and she can't say anything without admitting to arranging it all." I began to feel relieved as soon as I said it, realizing as I spoke that it was all true.

"We won't tell the police, Roger," Nicolle said.

"We'll tell your mother," Steve said.

It took me a second to take that in and respond. I assumed an incredulous expression, incredulous and dismissive. "You're going to *tell on me*, Steve? You're not serious."

"We're very serious, Roger," said Steve. "That's exactly what we'll do. We'll tell Ida that her son is the guy killing her friends."

I lost any semblance of nonchalance. "*You can't do that! Do you know what that would do to her?*"

"So don't make us do it," he said.

I remembered then, for the first time since I'd arrived, that I held something over them as well, that I hadn't come to this gunfight unarmed. Maybe all I'd brought was a knife, but it wasn't nothing. I eyed the two of them. "And what if I tell Larry you two are—"

"We still tell your mother," Steve said. "You can tell him whatever you want, and it'll suck for us, but there's only one way that your mother doesn't find out that her son is a bad, bad man."

"A monster," Nicolle added.

So much for my insurrection. I slumped back in my seat.

"It doesn't have to be like this, Roger," Nicolle said. "Even after I split that money with my brother, we'll have enough for you too. All Steven and I want is enough to get started. We would be pretty generous."

"Yeah," Steve said. "How long you want to live in your mother's basement anyway?"

Chapter Fifteen

I did not agree to do it, but I told them I would think about it, and drove home thinking about nothing else, until I remembered Max and Katrin and their grandmother, whereupon I would think about that awful, threatening situation until my mind was drawn back to the other one. Despite the cold air rushing in through the open window, my hands were sweaty on the steering wheel, my grip stiff and tight.

I arrived home a bit after five, the sky approaching full dark, to the alarming sight of the front door standing wide open while an ambulance drove away, its red and blue lights spinning. I leapt from the car, afraid something terrible had happened to my mother, not knowing whether to follow the ambulance or go inside.

From the doorway, my mother's friend Sylvia called out to me. "Roger, come in here before I freeze to death."

I rushed to the door, and Sylvia immediately said, "Don't worry. Your mother's fine. She fainted, but she was feeling much better by the time the ambulance got here."

"Where is she? Is she upstairs?" I asked and headed that way

"Calm down, Roger. She's in the ambulance. She wanted to send them away, but I insisted that she go in for tests, just in case."

"But why did she faint? Did they say what was wrong?"

"That's what the tests are for, aren't they?" she said, speaking to me as if I were a slow child. "Ida asked me to wait here for you, so you wouldn't worry. You can drive me to the hospital now and take her home when she's done. I'll have my grandson come pick me up after we hear what the doctors have to say."

THEY'D TAKEN her to a hospital in Bethpage, Sylvia told me, a ten-minute drive away. I glanced over at her, silent on the seat beside me as I got back on the Seaford Oyster Bay Expressway, remembered what had flashed through my mind when I'd seen Sylvia standing there in the doorway: She had found out about the pills from Max and Katrin, told my mother that I had killed their friend. I saw my mother grabbing at her chest, collapsing to the floor with the news.

"So, how are things with your new girlfriend?" she asked, turning to look at me after we'd been driving for a few minutes.

"Excuse me?" I said.

"Your mother tells me that you've been spending time with Gina Capitano's daughter."

"We're just friends," I said, gruffly. "Not that it's any of your business."

From the corner of my eye, I saw her smile.

"So that didn't work out either?"

"Thanks for your interest, Sylvia, but I don't think you have any idea what goes on in a modern relationship."

She snorted. "You think things are different now? You don't think I've known men like you my whole life?"

"What does that even mean, men like me? Where have you known men like me?"

"Here."

"What?"

"Turn here, the exit, coming up," she said pointing ahead.

I made the turn and was glad to let the subject drop when she didn't pursue it. Sylvia directed me the rest of the way to Saint Joseph's Hospital, where a nurse led us back through green-tiled corridors deeper into the building, to a small exam room where my mother sat upright on a crisp-sheeted bed. A nurse was just wheeling an EKG cart out of the room, and my mother was buttoning up the sweater she wore.

"How are you feeling, Mom?" I asked.

"They're making such a fuss!" she said.

"You can't be too careful at our age, Ida," Sylvia said. "Did the doctor tell you anything yet?"

"I haven't even seen a doctor! Just all his helpers and nurses," my mother said just as a sleek, starched doctor entered the room. He was a bit younger than me, looked exceedingly fit, and wore round steel spectacles that matched his neatly trimmed, steel-gray hair.

"Which of you two young ladies is Ida Faber?" he asked, smiling professionally.

Sylvia narrowed her eyes, and though it wasn't quite audible, I believe she might actually have sniffed in distaste.

"Ah, you must be the patient," he said to my mother, and I moved away as he stepped toward the bedside. He switched the clipboard he carried to his left hand, and held out his right for her to shake. "I'm Doctor Schneider."

My mother shook his hand and said, "Would you please tell these two that there's nothing to worry about?" He ignored her as he looked down at his charts, including a sheet of paper that had obviously just been ripped from the EKG machine. He flipped through a few pages beneath it.

"I understand that you're on—" he said, and rattled off a few medications.

"Yes, that's right," she said, a little anxiously.

"Did you start taking the"—unrecognizable name—"recently?"

"Yes, why?" my mother asked, now sounding a bit alarmed. "Doctor Frankel said that my blood pressure was too high, and that would fix it."

"You never told me about that," I said.

"I didn't want to worry you. It's nothing . . . Isn't that right, Doctor? It's nothing?"

"Well . . ." he said, and looked at the charts again. "Doctor Frankel is where?"

"He's my internist in Florida."

"Well, I'm sure Doctor Frankel knows what he's doing, but I think we need to make a few adjustments in your medication." He looked up from his papers and smiled at her. "All right?"

"Yes, of course, Doctor," my mother said, but she seemed flustered and upset now.

The doctor turned to me. "You're the son?"

"Yes."

"Could I speak to you for a moment?" He looked briefly at my mother and Sylvia. "If that's all right with you ladies." He didn't wait for them to answer, just walked out into the corridor. I followed.

"Mr. Faber, is it?"

"Olivetti," I said. "Roger Olivetti."

"Roger, I'm a bit concerned about your mother's heart. Her weight is a serious problem at her age, and the EKG's not excellent. With her low estrogen levels, she's in the sweet spot for a heart attack. She needs to eat better and start getting more exercise, for starters. I'd like to see her again in a few weeks."

"Is that why she fainted? Was it her heart?"

"No, not at all. She's on a new antihypertensive to lower her blood pressure. They brought it down a bit too low, and that brought on a syncope event."

"A what?"

"She fainted," he said, forbearingly.

"Will it happen again?"

"I can't predict the future, Roger. It's certainly possible. Driving might not be a good idea. Tell me, does your mother live with you or is she still independent?"

"Well, ah, she . . . she still lives in her own house."

"Maybe it's time you thought about moving her in with you, or hiring someone to come in and look after her."

"Okay," I said, but he didn't look up from what he was scribbling on the pad he had taken from his pocket.

"I want her to switch to these dosages on her blood-pressure medications," he said, handing me a stereotype-defyingly legible set of instructions. "But you also need to get her in better shape. And for the time being, keep her calm. Try to avoid anything that's too upsetting. Maybe keep her at home, where you can control the environment. She's not getting any younger, you know."

"So, that's it? We can go now?"

"Don't see why not," he said, then gave my hand one quick shake and began to turn away.

"Wait," I said. "Aren't you going to say anything else to my mother? She'd really—"

"I'm sure she'd rather hear it coming from you," he said, and hurried off to his next patient.

I returned to them as my mother was getting off the bed, leaning heavily on Sylvia as she did. As I watched, it occurred to me how often lately my mother would call out from the couch, "Come help me get up," or else work her way to her feet in slow, clumsy stages.

"Where's Dr. Schneider?" my mother asked. "Isn't he coming back?"

"No, he was in a hurry," I explained. "He told me everything. You're fine, Mom. We just have to start thinking about how you can be a little healthier."

"*What?* What's wrong with me?"

"Calm down, Ida," Sylvia said. "If it was anything serious, he would have told you himself." She turned to me. "This is what happens. You'll see. They start treating you like a child."

"I wouldn't say that, exactly," I said, but it did seem a bit irregular that I was now somehow in charge.

"Well, what did he say?" Sylvia asked. "Tell us."

"Nothing, really, but I think it would be good—the doctor thinks it would be good if you started exercising, and thought about, well, losing a little weight. Sorry, Mom." I held out the doctor's notes. "Here. He wants you to change the dosage of your medications."

She took the page from me, looked at it, then back up at me, looking lost, as if she'd discovered she could no longer read.

I reached out, took it back from her. "Don't worry about it. We'll go over it together at home."

Sylvia had opened the tall metal locker against the wall, took my mother's coat from the hanger, and helped her on with it.

"And maybe we should talk about getting somebody in to help you," I said.

"What? I don't need any help!" my mother protested. "You can help me if I need help."

"We'll talk about it, Mom. Come on, let's go home."

After we straightened out her insurance matters at the desk, I drove Sylvia to Harborside Manor, in North Massapequa, as her grandson had neither answered nor returned her calls. From what I could see, Harborside Manor was, as I had been repeatedly told, very nice. The grounds were pleasantly landscaped and well-maintained; what I could see through the windows of the lobby looked both homey and orderly; and the attendant that greeted Sylvia when she walked through the door seemed to have a genuine smile on her face.

When I finally got my mother home, she was very low-key, maybe a little bit in shock after what had happened. I told her to go sit and read, and I reheated some leftovers for our dinner. While we ate, I casually brought up the matter of a home healthcare aide, but she refused to even consider it.

"I don't want a stranger in my house, Roger! I don't need one. I have you."

I HAD never really given much thought to my mother's health. Husbands dropped dead on her, left and right, but she had always plowed steadily forward, like a broad and ponderous cruise ship, slowly and unstoppably cutting through the waves. I knew, of course, that this could not go on indefinitely, but her death had always seemed so far in the future that it had no relevance to the present. If you'd asked me that morning, and I'd been forced to think about it, I would have guessed she had another ten years at least, possibly twenty.

I know I might have presented myself as unsentimental, but when all is said and done I am subject to the same emotional calculus as anyone else, the inverse square law that left you unmoved by the death of a distant stranger, while it was impossible to escape the pull of those who were close to you. I did not want my mother to die.

In the diner, when Steve and Nicolle had threatened to speak to her, tell her the things I had done, I had been worried about what she would think of me, how upset she would be. I could attempt to explain it all to her, of course, explain that I had never really had any choice. I could attempt to explain, even, that none of us have any choice, that we were all carried along by an infinite number of intersecting currents, unseen beneath the surface; that we shouted our intentions into the wind and thought we heard assent when they blew back in our faces; that we dipped our paddles in attempting to steer, but at best avoided capsizing. I could explain all that, but I could not expect her to understand, could in fact count on her not to. "Stop saying nonsense things!" she would say. "You killed my friends!"

But now Steve and Nicolle weren't just threatening to upset my mother, to tarnish her picture of me, they were threatening her life. A failing heart and the sudden revelation that your son is a serial killer do not pair well. I had been appalled when Lisa proposed I consider cold-blooded murder for money, and was not tempted when Steve and Nicolle offered to pay me to kill Larry, but this wasn't about money any longer. This was a matter of protecting my mother, just as killing Mary Mahoney had been something I'd done to protect myself.

And Larry was, really, exactly as they had presented him. He was a racist and a misogynist, and ultimately a thug, a criminal. Even if he'd never committed a violent act himself, he was complicit. He had gotten where he was through his conscious association with people whose tactics involved the extralegal application of violence.

I'm not going to pretend I'm not also complicit in violence. We all are. Anyone who lives in a stable society enjoys that stability only because of the implicit violence of the state. The state is made of violence; violence is its very substance. Laws are obeyed because if they are not, the state will effectuate some tiny amount of that unrealized violence and bring it to bear against you. We can only go about our lives, rubbing up against each other with all our conflicting goals and inevitable conflicts, because we have agreed to turn violence over to the state. We are protected by that violence, and thus we bear responsibility for it, but we have given up the right to decide to be violent ourselves.

People like Larry, his colleagues in New York, were like rats in the woodwork of society; staying just hidden enough to go about their violent business unregulated and unhindered. But by living the sort of life he lived, stepping outside the laws that took the option of violence away from individuals, Larry had declined the protection of those laws, voided the user agreement we all opted into by default, and made himself fair game.

And, okay, if I'm being completely honest, I had never quite reconciled myself to the awfulness of his writing. There was a time not that long ago when being a writer was something special. My novels might not have been successful, but they exhibited a certain level of skill and professionalism, and just as importantly, a knowledge of literature and the humanistic values it conveyed that came from years of thoughtful reading. Now, someone like Larry, someone who had probably never read anything that didn't *gain* depth when it was made into a Hollywood movie, churned out book after book, self-published them, and called himself an author. I will never stop finding that galling, and while the case against him was written in his character and his actions, it could be found just as clearly in his writing.

That was beside the point, of course. You could not justify killing someone just because he was an awful writer— the streets would run with rivers of blood. The only real question was whether his life outweighed the risk of letting Steve and Nicolle tell my mother something that might put her in her grave. It was his life or hers.

What were my options? Turn them in? They had not done anything the police could act on. It was their word against mine, and there was a good chance that reporting them would end with me in jail, which was no less likely to kill my mother. Kill them instead? That was absurd, and surely ending Larry's life was the lesser wrong. Simply run away? There was no guarantee that if I did they would not tell her about me anyway.

I had been hoping to leave and start over somewhere else with the money I got from Brad. I had been ignoring it, didn't want to let it influence me, but I was not unaware that with what I might get from Steve and Nicolle on top of that, my new life in a second-rate city would start out that much better.

I picked up the phone and dialed. When Steve answered, I asked, "How much?"

CHAPTER SIXTEEN

Most evenings, after the day's work, Larry drove out to Jones Beach alone, where he'd stare out at the ocean and think his thoughts about the future, about his novels, about whatever it was somebody like Larry might think about while contemplating the vast and restless sea. This time of year, deep in winter, by five or six the sky was dark, the beaches abandoned by even the hardiest walkers and metal detectors, the parking lots empty. This, Steve told me, is where I should do it.

My father's Korean War sidearm, an M1911 pistol, which you'll remember from the first act, had a full magazine, something I was able to ascertain after watching a few instructional videos on YouTube. The action was stiff, but those same videos showed me how to take it entirely apart, oil its various mechanisms, and reassemble it into a perfectly functional weapon. I briefly considered surreptitiously borrowing my mother's handgun, as it was newer and presumably less prone to misfires and accidents, but that would add risks that did not seem worth it. A bullet fired from my mother's gun would be more easily traceable than sixty-year-old army-issue ammunition, and if I disposed of the gun afterward, as I planned to, and it was subsequently somehow found, there would be a record of who it had been sold to, and it would not take long for that record to lead to me.

There was no need for me to take the gun out somewhere and practice shooting cans off a fence, or anything like that. If this was to work, it would work because Larry knew me and trusted me, and I would be standing right next to him when I did it. Even a novice like myself, somebody who had never before fired a gun, was not likely to miss from a distance of eighteen inches.

Those preparations were simple enough, but I still hesitated to go through with it. I spent days doing little but work on my novel and make sure my mother was taking the right combination of pills at the right time of day. I wrote out in large, block script all the times and dosages for her, and set alarms on my phone to remind me to remind her. More often than not, when the intrusive chirruping of my phone came, it would find me in the world of my book, the increasingly rich and detailed fiction I was creating.

Another thing I did was paste a signature file into the proper field on the final page of the pdf contract for Brad's book, type in the date, and email the document to his assistant; she emailed back to tell me I would receive a check for fifty thousand dollars within two weeks. Added to the hundred thousand I would be getting from Steve and Nicolle, I was looking forward to starting my new life quite comfortably.

Only two things stood in my way. The first was my mother. She needed someone to look after her, and I had not yet brought her around to agreeing that a hired aide would be just as good—better—than me. The other, of course, was following through on my agreement with Steve and Nicolle.

ON A clear, cold evening, I went upstairs to make sure my mother had taken her pills, then told her I would be going out for a while. I took her car keys—now kept on the kitchen counter; I had taken on the job of driving her where she needed to go and, with it, de facto control of her car—and left the house with my father's gun, oiled and loaded, in the deep side pocket of my down coat.

I backed the car out of the driveway, headlights sweeping the front of the house as I turned into the street. Steve and Nicolle knew where Larry liked to go, one of the westernmost parking lots on the long barrier island that made up Jones Beach. Though I hadn't been there in thirty years, I knew the way. I knew it the way you remember the music of your youth, laid down when the clay was soft and almost leapt up to embrace whatever might make an impression. All through my teen years I had driven to Jones Beach, first in the back seat of somebody else's car, and later behind the wheel myself. It was where we went to drink and party, to lie entangled together on blankets at night, our big backyard. We went there to escape adult supervision, but we were drawn just as much by the atavistic urge to be in something like nature. And despite the parties and the drinking and the fumbling sex, I'd always found it calming to look out over the sand to the ocean, to see a big sky without the clutter of the suburbs beneath it. Even the drive there was calming to me. Now, as I got on Wantagh State Parkway and headed south, the fifteen-minute drive taking me from faceless neighborhoods—the lights of other cars growing fewer around me as I went—to a causeway bordered by nothing but stretches of scrubby growth and saltwater inlets, I relaxed into my task.

I reached the roundabout at the entrance of Jones Beach State Park proper and headed west along the road that took me past the series of parking lots that gave access to the beach. On a summer day, cars would be bumper to bumper here, the parking lots full, everything hectic with teens and families eager to spread blankets on the beach, become part of the checkerboard of skin and sand that stretched from the grassy dunes down to the waterline. Now it was abandoned, a ghost town, and I was free to cruise slowly along, scan each parking lot I passed, looking for Larry's—hopefully—lone car.

I found him in the last parking lot at the very west end of the beach. Sitting behind the weather-worn bathhouse were a couple of maintenance vehicles, beat-up pickups with JONES BEACH STATE PARK stenciled on their doors. They, like the bathhouse, were dark, with no signs of life around them. Otherwise, the parking lot, vast to accommodate the summer hordes, was deserted but for Larry, a small figure leaning back against the hood of his sleek BMW.

I drove slowly toward him, and could see him turn to look my way as I parked the car twenty yards away. I was close enough to make out a look of concern at being disturbed here, his personal retreat. Once I got out and he could see me, his expression turned clearly to pleasure.

"Roger! You finally decided to come join me! How'd you find me?"

"Hey, Larry. Steve told me where to look."

He patted the hood next to him with a leather-gloved hand, slid over from the center to give me some room. I stationed myself there, to the right of him, leaned back, and the two of us looked out across the beach. The night was cloudless, and there was enough light from a near-full moon to render the beach pale, the water line distinct as each dark wave broke on the shore a hundred yards away, its frothy edge racing up the sand and then retreating again. I had my hands in my coat pockets, my right clamped tightly around the grip of the gun.

"You get everything worked out with Roman?" Larry asked casually, as if it were some minor paperwork I'd had to deal with.

"Yeah. It's all taken care of."

"I knew you'd figure something out," he said. "Glad it wasn't too much trouble."

"Thanks," I said, and I felt my hand growing sweaty in the warmth of my pocket. There was no reason to put this off; it would make no real difference if he lived for a few more minutes or not, and yet I found myself saying, "So, how's the new book coming?"

"Great!" he said. "I really think this one's going to be special. See, I decided to write this one from the POV of, get this, not the hero, but the hero's friend, so it's a whole new way to tell the story." He looked my way, expectant.

"That's pretty clever," I said.

"It's funny, too! Because this guy, the friend? He's not so good at a lot of the stuff the main guy is good at, and it's, like, a contrast between them. And he's not that smart, so sometimes when he tells you something? It's not always true! Because he's wrong! And you hafta figure that out. I'm telling ya, Roger, I really think this is going to be my breakthrough book."

"Sounds like it," I said. Despite himself, Larry was getting better. He had stumbled onto the unreliable narrator. Certainly not a new idea, but it would add some much-needed depth to the two-dimensional material he'd been churning out— But what was I thinking? He would never finish it.

I began to slowly draw the gun out of my pocket, when Larry said, "Hey, what are you working on, Roger? Been meaning to ask you about that. It's been years since I've seen a new book from you. You hang up your writer's hat for good?"

"Actually, no. I'm working on something now."

"Oh, yeah? I bet it's great. What is it?"

This was starting to get a bit too chummy for my taste, given what I was there for, and I knew it was time to get it over with, before we got any deeper into this conversation, before I could grow any more conflicted. He was now looking at me expectantly, though, and I could not bring myself to do it when he could see what was coming. I wanted him to be looking away, out to sea; I wanted it to happen before he knew it was happening, and so I found myself telling him about my novel. Besides, I still didn't have anyone to talk to about it.

Larry responded enthusiastically, nodding his head in encouragement, throwing me "Wow"s and "Ha"s. When I was done, he shook his head in appreciation, and turned to look back out at the ocean. "You know, Roger," he said, "I'm a good writer, but I don't think I'll ever be able to write like you do. Me, I just do it 'cause I love it, but I gotta hand it to you. You're a real professional."

"Thanks," I said, and lifted the gun fully from my pocket, held it down by my side, away from him.

"Can I tell you something, Roger?"

"Sure, Larry."

"Look out there," he said, and pointed at the horizon. "You know what I see? A cruise ship."

I looked. I saw no cruise ship.

"Where?" I asked, and began to raise the gun.

He turned to me again, a little impatient. He did not, fortunately, look down. "Not now. Someday. I'm gonna set up a gambling ship. I've been planning this for years. I don't want to just be in the restaurant business. I mean, that's okay, it's been good to me, but I don't just want to be the same guy when I retire that my father was when he retired, end up the same place I started. I want to do something bigger than that. I almost have the money now. It'll just be another couple years. It's gonna be great, Roger. It'll have everything. Bars, music. Room full of slots. I'm gonna spare no expense. People'll dress up. There'll be dancing and dinner until we get out to the three-mile line, and then it'll be just like an Atlantic City casino. It'll be really classy, Roger."

He sighed and stared out over the water.

"So, what do you think?" he asked me, as I got ready, steeled myself.

In my head, I pictured it, me pointing the gun right at his head, pulling the trigger. His body slumping, falling to the ground. Me standing over him, looking down at his corpse, his dreams extinguished along with his life.

I just couldn't do it. He could have been Gatsby, looking out at his green light, dreaming of a future where money had transformed him into someone else, freed him from his past, from himself. He might be a base, talentless, racist thug, but in his own way, he was trying to better himself, move up, live a better life. Could I really condemn him because his idea of a better life was different than mine, if his idea of how he was supposed to get there didn't follow the rules I thought were appropriate? He had been following the path laid out for him, just like the rest of us, using the tools at hand, heading toward the vision he was equipped to see.

And how could I condemn him for his self-published novels? He wanted to be an author; thought it was a better thing to be, a higher plane of existence. He'd done his best, banged on the door, petitioned the gatekeepers, but he'd been turned away. He couldn't see why, wasn't equipped to, Dunning-Krugered into never understanding. When the gates had been stormed, when Amazon had thrown open the back door, was it really so wrong for him to rush in and plant his flag?

I could no longer remember how I had convinced myself that he deserved to die. I had agreed to do it because it seemed to me that I had no choice. I would make a choice now.

I slipped the gun back into my pocket.

"I think it sounds great, Larry. Real classy."

DURING THE drive home, I figured it out, how I could make this work. I would write Brad's damn book, and give the money to Steve and Nicolle. I would keep just enough to live on. It wasn't as much as they were hoping for, but maybe it would be enough for them to get started, enough for them to drop this insane plan. They weren't bad people. For them, killing Larry wasn't a goal; it was a means to an end, and if I could offer them some other means, I was sure they would eventually accept it. They might even be relieved.

I'd have to work on Brad's book for at least six months, maybe a year, but if I could move somewhere pleasant, somewhere I didn't feel so surrounded, somewhere that wasn't my mother's basement, it would be bearable. Rochester, Minnesota. Boise, Idaho. Eugene, Oregon. I could work with Brad by email, by Skype. My mother would just have to accept that I wouldn't be there to take care of her. I still had a life ahead of me and it started with doing the right thing. I wasn't going to sacrifice that to her aversion to having a stranger in the house.

WHEN I got out of the car at my mother's house, the light was on in the living room. I resolved to tell my mother right then that I would be leaving. The sooner that was out of the way, the sooner I could start making plans, start fixing things. When I opened the front door and stepped in, though, she was not alone.

My mother was in her favorite spot, on the couch next to her crystal swan. Sitting beside her was Sylvia, who smiled at me, lifted her hand from her lap, and pointed my mother's gun at me.

"Hello, Roger," Sylvia said. "We've been waiting for you."

"Mom," I said, without taking my eyes off Sylvia, "why is Sylvia pointing your gun at me?"

"Roger," my mother said, "Sylvia has been telling me some very upsetting things about you."

"Shut the door, Roger," Sylvia said. "We need to have a talk."

I shut the door behind me. Despite the many times I had imagined everything going wrong, I had not imagined that it might look like this. Cops showing up at the door, roughly handcuffing me, taking me in, yes. Mob goons driving me out to the Pine Barrens, chatting like everything was just fine; as unlikely as it was, I'd imagined that too. But Sylvia and my mother, at gunpoint? No, that hadn't occurred to me.

"About what?" I asked.

"I think you know, Roger, but fine, have it your way," Sylvia said. "Were you at Mary Mahoney's house the day we had our book club meeting there?"

"Mary who?" I said, not as convincingly as I might have hoped.

"My granddaughter Katrin tells me you had Mary's pills with you when she saw you later that day."

"What? Those? I bought them from some kids in the street, Sylvia. For my toe. I'm not proud of it, but I was in a lot of pain. It doesn't mean anything." I sounded so unconvincing, even to myself, that I wanted to ask if I could try again.

"Oh, Roger," my mother said, taking out a handkerchief from her bag and blotting her eyes as she started to cry. "How can you lie to your mother?"

"Explain something else to me, Roger," Sylvia continued. "Irene Baranski told your mother she saw you at Lisa Capitano's house the day of her mother's funeral."

"Yes, so? I was paying my respects to Mrs. Capitano, Sylvia. She meant a lot to me."

"But your mother tells me you didn't come out here from the city until that night. How did you pay your respects if you weren't here yet?"

"I, uh, I—"

"You were already staying here when Gina Capitano died, Roger," Sylvia said with complete certainty, and I could hear in her voice both prosecutor and judge; could hear in her conviction my own.

Well, fine then. I had a gun too. If it came to it, I would not let Sylvia send me to jail. I reached into my coat pocket. Was this what I would have to do? Would I have to shoot my mother's friend, right in front of her? Would she ever forgive me for that? I would have to make her see that I'd had no choice.

"You couldn't call and tell me you were staying here?" my mother said through her tears. "You know I would have come up if you needed me."

"Hush, Ida. That doesn't matter right now," Sylvia said.

"Don't you hush me, Sylvia! It does matter! If I'd been here for him, he would never have done these horrible things," my mother said.

While they were occupied squabbling with each other, I took out the gun, aimed it at Sylvia.

"Okay," I said, interrupting them. "Enough. Put down the gun, Sylvia."

They both looked at me then, surprised and, for just a moment, speechless. Then my mother squinted through her glasses and said, "Is that the gun from the basement?"

"Yes, Mom. It's the gun from the basement. Sylvia, put your gun down."

My mother sat up straight and said, "You know you're not allowed to play with that, Roger! It's not a toy! You give that to me!" Her tears gone now, my mother, determined to take the gun away from me, hurried to get up from the couch, but she was no longer built to do anything in a hurry, least of all get up from the couch, and she struggled like a beetle on its back. "And stop pointing it at Sylvia!"

"But, Mom, Sylvia's pointing a gun at *me*!" I said, as she finally managed to lever herself to her feet.

"I don't care what Sylvia's doing! If Sylvia jumped off a bridge, would you jump off a bridge too? *Stop pointing a gun at Sylvia!*" she said, shaking a finger at me. She started toward me, took two steps, and without preamble, fainted again.

As she began to fall forward I instinctively tried to catch her, and as I reached out to break her fall I must have squeezed the trigger, because that is when the gun finally, inevitably, went off.

When I saw what I had done, I realized that no matter what I might tell myself, this was something my mother would never forgive me for, something she would never get over.

WHEN MY mother came to and sat up a few minutes later, she saw what had happened and gasped.

"You shot my crystal swan!" she screamed, sounding, if anything, more upset than she'd been before.

"Relax, Ida," Sylvia said. "We'll get you a new one. I think they're on sale now anyway."

There were shards of glass all over, except on the couch, where Sylvia had brushed them away before I lifted my mother up to carry her over and lay her carefully down. While I had been doing that, Sylvia had the presence of mind to retrieve the gun I had dropped on the floor in my confusion and concern. She now had both guns, and after directing me to go to the kitchen to fetch a damp cloth to lay across my mother's forehead, she stood with one of them trained on me.

My options exhausted, I said, "Are you going to turn me in?"

"So you admit it? That you killed them?" Sylvia asked as she sat back down next to my mother.

I didn't see any way around it. They already knew. "Yes. Yes, I did it."

"How could you, Roger?" my mother said. "I didn't raise you to kill people. What were you going to do next? Assassinate the president?"

"Mom, you don't understand. It wasn't like that."

"Why don't you tell us what it was like, Roger," Sylvia said.

"I never meant to hurt anyone. I was tricked. I was manipulated, I was—"

"Only following orders?" Sylvia volunteered.

"That's not fair. It's not the same thing. It wasn't my idea! I had no choice."

Sylvia set the gun down on the couch next to her. "I know, Roger," she said.

"You do?" I couldn't have been more surprised. I'd never really expected anyone to understand, least of all somebody who seemed as unsympathetic toward me as Sylvia.

"I told you I've known men like you all my life. You would never do something like that on your own. You don't have the—" She stopped, silenced by her own unwillingness to say something so vulgar out loud.

My mother leaned forward. "*The balls,*" she supplied, in her loud, showy whisper.

"I've known that minx Lisa Capitano all her life," Sylvia continued. "She's always been trouble. This is exactly the kind of thing she'd do. It's obvious she was leading you around by—"

"*Your little thingy,*" my mother loud-whispered again, interrupting, nodding in a knowing way.

"The *nose*, Ida. I was going to say the nose."

"You were very bad, Roger," my mother said, brushing aside Sylvia's excuses for me.

"I know, Mom."

"I want you to promise me that you won't kill any more of my friends."

"I won't, Mom, I promise," I said.

"None of them! Do you understand me? Not one more!"

"Yes, Mom, I understand."

"See, Sylvia, we don't have to worry." Now that she'd resolved this to her satisfaction, I could see my mother righting herself, like one of those round-bottomed clown balloons that spring back up no matter how many times you knock them over. I could almost hear her thinking *See! He's a good boy!*

"I wasn't worried, Ida," said Sylvia.

"So you're *not* going to turn me in?" I asked.

"No, Roger," Sylvia said. "It would break your mother's heart if you went to jail. We're not going to do that unless we have to."

A wash of relief immediately passed through me, and almost as immediately vanished.

"What does that mean, unless you have to?"

"Roger, your mother isn't well—"

"I'm fine, Sylvia," my mother said. "Stop saying that."

"I'm sorry, Ida, but we both know you need somebody to look after you now. You just fainted again! Roger, I know you weren't planning to stay in your mother's basement forever, but you're going to have to put aside any plans you were making. Your mother needs somebody here, and you're going to stay. You'll take her to her appointments, make sure she takes her medication, do the shopping, drive her where she needs to go. She's going to need more help as time goes on, and you're going to stay here and make sure she has it."

I could hear doors slamming shut, one after another. Nashville, Tennessee. Bangor, Maine. Chapel Hill, North Carolina.

"Roger, don't look so upset!" my mother said. "You won't have to look after me forever."

"Mom," I said, automatically, "don't say that. You're not dying anytime soon."

"Bite your tongue, Roger! That's not what I meant at all. Sylvia got me on the waiting list at Harborside. She pulled some strings, didn't you, Sylvia?"

"I did," Sylvia said. "You only have to help your mother out until a unit opens up, Roger. It would be nice if you'd stay after that, and come visit your mother regularly, but if you're willing to show us we can depend on you, we wouldn't say anything."

"I'd never hurt anybody else! Just now, at the beach, I—" I cut myself off. Not killing Larry wasn't that strong a testament to my character.

Sylvia looked at me curiously, waited for me to continue, and when I didn't, said "Hmmph. We'll see about that. Anyway, if you'll stay here and take care of your mother until we can get her into Harborside Manor, we can keep all of this to ourselves."

Fine. I could do this. I still had my novel to work on. I could handle staying here as long as I had that, something that was truly mine. I could live in my mother's basement and take care of her, and write about Brad's dick, as long as I knew I had something of my own, that one freedom. And maybe it would all work out. Maybe, if I could get the novel finished, when this was over, when I left here—

"Oh, and you know what I was thinking, Roger?" my mother said. "As long as you're going to be staying here, you could finally take the time to read Morris's novel, and

see if you can find somebody to publish it!" She turned to
Sylvia. "You should read it too! I think you'd like it."

"Ida, I read it," said Sylvia. "You gave it to me. I'm sorry,
but it's not a good book."

"But it's so clever!" My mother turned to me. "It's all
about reincarnation."

Oh, that's right, I recalled. Funny coincidence too. *My*
novel was about reincarnation. A chill ran through me then,
as I suddenly understood that it wasn't a coincidence at all.

I was writing Morris's novel. It had gotten into my head
and I'd forgotten where it had come from. The entire structure was the same. I leaned back against the wall, slowly
slid down until I was seated on the floor. The lies Darius
had spread about me, had sent out into the world to ruin
me—I'd turned them into the truth. I had stolen Morris's
idea.

"Roger, are you all right?" my mother asked, looking a
little alarmed.

"No, mom. I'm not all right."

"Stop being so dramatic," Sylvia said. "You only have to
stay here until one of the other residents dies."

I looked at them, then, at the two old ladies sitting side
by side on the couch, and Sylvia smiled at me. "Of course,"
she said, "it would be that much sooner if something were
to happen to Mr. Pedone . . ."

Epilogue

You'll be wanting closure on all this, of course. You're still here because you want to know if I decided to kill Mr. Pedone; if I threw away whatever progress I might have made toward redeeming myself when I chose not to kill Larry; if self-interest finally drove me to let go of any illusions I was still holding on to about who I was and what I would and would not do.

I imagine, though, that you're hoping I refused. There must have been a few moments during all this when I seemed at least a little likable, a slightly sympathetic character, so it's only natural you'd want to hear that I learned something from my experiences, decided to maintain the line I'd drawn in the sand that night on the beach, the principled stand I'd taken when I turned down Lisa's last business proposition.

So, which was it, do you think? Did I selfishly buy my freedom at the cost of another's life, or did I accept my Long Island exile as just punishment for my sins and allow the door of my basement prison to clang unmistakably shut?

I honestly wish I could tell you, because I'd like to know too.

The thing is, the decision was taken out of my hands. Three weeks later, while I was still agonizing about it, immobilized between two distinctly different but equally awful bales of hay, word reached me that Mr. Pedone had died in his sleep, of natural causes. Natural natural causes.

I can't even tell you what I would have done if he hadn't died, because I no longer believe anyone knows what they're capable of doing until they've already done it and they can look back and see. And even if I could look back and see, we'd still never really know the truth of it, because I'd inevitably make up a story about whatever it was I saw, first to explain it to myself, and then to convince anyone else who would listen to see it my way. It would no doubt be a story with justice, or redemption, or maybe both, because I know people like that, and I would probably be the hero, because, well, I would like that, and there'd definitely be closure, because who doesn't want closure?

Those are the kinds of stories we tell each other, the kind we tell ourselves. We want our stories to be well shaped and satisfying, we want them to have arcs, and beginnings and endings. We want characters who do the right thing, and are rewarded for it, so we can identify with them, or characters who do the wrong thing and suffer the consequences, so we can shiver and congratulate ourselves because that would never happen to us, or characters who start out bad, but learn and grow, so we can do both. Most of all, and at a minimum, we want our stories to make sense.

Unfortunately, like I said, I can't give you any of that, so I'm just going to have to tell you what really happened, and what really happens seldom features justice, or redemption, or closure, and it only ever makes sense when we squint at it just right and ignore the parts that don't.

What happened is that everything worked out pretty well for me. Not long after Mr. Pedone died, my mother took his place in Harborside Manor, where, you'll be glad to hear, she's very happy. Once she settled in, she decided to give me the house, and I had Lisa put it on the market.

It sold quickly, and I put some of the money into Steve and Nicolle's new restaurant, which shows every sign of being a smart investment. I considered buying a place—I could just about afford a studio in Queens—but not long after Mr. Pedone died, I got a call from Anna.

Remember Anna, from the train? I had been so caught up in worrying about my performance in bed that it had obscured the fact that we'd genuinely hit it off. She got tired of waiting to hear from me and took the initiative. We went out to dinner a few times, got to know each other a bit, one thing led to another, and eventually I moved in. Now Anna commutes into the city to work, while I stay home and take care of things around the house. As for my performance issues, that all sorted itself out as soon as I began to feel at home here and it stopped being a performance.

Speaking of which, I never wrote a word of Brad's book. The day before our first scheduled meeting, Elanie called to cancel. Brad had gotten involved in some new foundation he'd started with Bono, and he was all caught up in saving the world, or something along those lines. I'm not really up on the details. The important thing is that he lost interest in becoming an author.

I got to keep the first check, which was nice of course, but this also meant I'd lost my ticket back to the bestseller lists, and that left me adrift for a while. Eventually, though, with time on my hands and enough money that it wasn't a pressing issue, I got back to work on my novel. Yes, I got the idea from Morris, and sure, that threw me at first, but everything comes from somewhere, and no matter how we try to escape where we come from, we carry it with us forever. No matter where you go, etc.; boats, current, ceaseless past, blah, blah, blah. It's something you learn to live with.

Sarah and I fell out of touch once the divorce was final, and it sort of goes without saying that she got to keep all our friends. I don't really blame them. I mean, come on. I would have picked her too. But with Anna in the city all day, there was nobody I could talk to about my novel, so, the thing is, I ended up hanging out with Larry some. I know, I know. He's not perfect, but who is? Certainly not me. Besides, nobody else has ever been so enthusiastic about my writing. It can make up for a lot.

Unfortunately, Darius was still nursing a grudge when I finished the book, and I *still* couldn't get anyone to get back to me. In the end, Larry convinced me to self-publish it on Amazon. I was reluctant at first, as I'm sure you can imagine, and it took me a while to get used to the idea, but Larry's right. Things are different these days, and lots of self-published novels are getting on the bestseller lists. Who knows, maybe this will be my breakthrough book.

ACKNOWLEDGMENTS

Traditionally, this is where you acknowledge all the arts institutions that awarded you residencies while you were writing your novel, places you went to work among other writers who value writing as much as you do, exchanging pages and receiving critiques that make you throw up your hands in despair of ever being understood, until you realize they have a point; muttering when they make too much noise, but getting together later for great conversation, jokes that you're still laughing at days later, late-night carousing, and wild affairs. The applications to those programs are a lot of work, though, and I hear you have to know somebody anyway. Fortunately, I got all of that when I met and eventually married Sandra Newman, so I will mention her here instead.

Thanks are due to Peternelle van Arsdale, an incisive editor and a good friend, whose thoughtful notes on an early version of this novel pointed the way to writing a better one. Thanks too, to Dr. Wayne Whitwam, M.D., who advised me on how to get away with killing old ladies, and also how to make them faint. Needless to say, he is not responsible for anything I did with that information thereafter.

Finally, to any family or friends on Long Island who read this, I acknowledge that this does not look good for me. Please remember that Roger is proven wrong about almost everything. His opinions are not mine, and none of the characters in this book are meant to reflect on any of you, although I did give Steve Campbell a bit of the unflappable, laconic cool I have often observed in my brother, Lewis.